FORBIDDEN TO THE MILLIONAIRE DOC

JULIETTE HYLAND

Harlequin

MEDICAL ROMANCE

Harlequin®
MEDICAL
ROMANCE

Recycling programs for this product may not exist in your area

ISBN-13: 978-1-335-99330-4

Forbidden to the Millionaire Doc

Copyright © 2025 by Juliette Hyland

For questions and comments about the quality of this book, please contact us at CustomerService@Harlequin.com.

TM and ® are trademarks of Harlequin Enterprises ULC.

Harlequin Enterprises ULC
22 Adelaide St. West, 41st Floor
Toronto, Ontario M5H 4E3, Canada
www.Harlequin.com

HarperCollins Publishers
Macken House, 39/40 Mayor Street Upper
Dublin 1, D01 C9W8, Ireland
www.HarperCollins.com

Printed in U.S.A.

Juliette Hyland began crafting heroes and heroines in high school. She lives in Ohio with her Prince Charming, who has patiently listened to many rants regarding characters failing to follow the outline. When not working on fun and flirty happily-ever-afters, Juliette can be found spending time with her beautiful daughters, giant dogs or sewing uneven stitches with her sewing machine.

Books by Juliette Hyland

Harlequin Medical Romance

Alaska Emergency Docs

One-Night Baby with Her Best Friend

Boston Christmas Miracles

A Puppy on the 34th Ward

Hope Hospital Surgeons

Dating His Irresistible Rival
Her Secret Baby Confession

Jet Set Docs

ER Doc's South Pole Reunion

Fake Dating the Vet

Harlequin Romance

Falling for His Fake Date

If the Fairy Tale Fits...

Beauty and the Brooding CEO

Visit the Author Profile page
at Harlequin.com for more titles.

For Bianca...welcome to the world.

San Diego Surgeons

Love in the city!

Welcome to San Diego! Sitting on the Pacific coast, the city's world-famous beaches make it the perfect destination for a sunshine getaway. But for Seth and Wren, the place tourists call paradise is also their home! And as surgeons at San Diego's leading hospital, they're the beating heart of the operating theaters. Now it's love that will set their own pulses racing...

When physical therapist Therese's heart is left shattered by her—now ex!—fiancé, surgeon Seth is the first person she turns to. They've been best friends *forever* and Therese seeks comfort in their unbreakable bond. But when it leads to an unexpected night of passion, they're wholly unprepared for the consequences...

Dr. Luca fiercely guards his heart, as well as the secret of his million-dollar fortune! But the arrival of sunshine surgeon Wren soon has his sky-high emotional walls crumbling, even though his best friend's sister should remain *firmly* off-limits...

Escape to San Diego with...

Expecting Her Best Friend's Baby by Tina Beckett

Forbidden to the Millionaire Doc by Juliette Hyland

Available now!

Dear Reader,

I grew up watching episodes of *Doogie Howser, M.D.* The idea of a genius child doctor was the foundation for my heroine. Wren didn't start med school at ten like Doogie, though she is still a teen when she hits those hallowed halls.

Dr. Wren Freson has a life no one else can imagine. A childhood genius who graduated high school at twelve, college at sixteen and med school at twenty, she has always felt like she doesn't quite belong. At twenty-eight she's determined to have her own life and is starting over in San Diego. The only thing she isn't ready for is falling for a blast from her past in the shape of her brother's former best friend.

Physical therapist Luca McDonnell is hot, good at his job and standoffish! The hospital faculty calls him McSteamy. No one knows the man well, but when Wren shows up, McSteamy transforms into the playful, fun man he used to be. But Luca has a secret and when anyone finds out, he loses them completely. Can he keep Wren, or will she be one more person he loses along the way?

Enjoy Wren and Luca's path to forever!

Juliette Hyland

CHAPTER ONE

DR. WREN FRESON counted to ten to keep herself from bouncing with glee as she stood in the center of the San Diego Central Library. Growing up, libraries were her refuge. A place she didn't feel gawked at for reading well above her grade level. At five, she'd meticulously read her way through the fantasy section. Then the ocean life section, so she could impress her big brother. This marked sixty-seven on her ever-growing list of libraries she'd visited around the country.

It was a silly thing her brother, Ronan, used to make fun of her for. No matter the city, she always visited the library. Or libraries. It was a task made easier by seeing as many of her brother's minor league baseball games around the country as possible. She'd been in tiny libraries and palatial ones. But this nine-story beauty was the most breathtaking she'd visited yet.

Since Wren had accepted the position of plastic surgeon for the burn unit at Sunrise Medical, this was also now her library. She patted her purse where the shiny new library card sat. She always had at least three books on her bedside table, usually ones her current patients were interested in.

Today she was here for another purpose.

She pursed her lips and pulled a baseball card from her purse. Ronan's grin brought a smile to her face, but the ache of knowing she only saw him in photos never truly went away. Her brother had lived and breathed baseball. Or he had, before he'd died in a car accident.

Three days away from his dream. He'd just been traded to a team that planned to start him in the majors. An accident stole it all from him and two other players in the car with him. That night had also stolen away the only person who ever truly saw her.

Her brother hadn't cared about her IQ. Didn't lead off every introduction with, *This is my sister, the genius.* He'd talk about his fish, her current schoolwork and gripe with her about their overbearing parents.

Her eyes misted, but she was not giving into tears. This was a happy moment. She was finally here. Heading for the elevators, she stepped on and got off on the eighth floor. The Sullivan Baseball Research Center. The largest baseball history research collection in the United States. In the world.

It had opened just before her brother started high school. When Wren, a *happy accident* according to her parents, was five. Ronan had talked about it constantly. His favorite topic was how one day he'd be in the records here.

That day was never coming, but she owed it to him to let this moment be his.

Walking into the research center, she smiled at all the baseball references decorating the walls. This was not a memorabilia collection; it was a *research center* dedicated to the history of the game. It was where authors came to dive into the deep lore for their books. Something Ronan had told their father more than once. Not that the man was ever interested in their interests.

Her parents had looked at her love of oceanography as a hurdle to get over as she headed for med school. And baseball—that was not something they'd ever enjoyed. They went to Ronan's senior year games because he was a starter; the other years—the benchwarmer years—they'd ignored.

Her parents were impressed by accomplishments. If Ronan had debuted in the majors, they'd have gone to every game. Bragging to anyone who got close to them. But when you weren't at the top, they weren't interested.

And they got to determine what *the top* meant.

She held the baseball card against her heart as she walked through the area. Wren didn't care about baseball. But she'd loved Ronan more than anything.

"I made it," she whispered to her brother. Hopefully his spirit knew his minor league card was wandering the research center.

Turning down one stack, she saw a dark-haired white man sitting at a table by a window. Her breath caught, and Wren blinked.

Luca? Luca McDonnell?

Wren blinked several more times as the name reverberated in her brain. This was a mirage. A fantasy conjured by her brain while she was remembering her brother. There was no way. *No way.* Luca wasn't in San Diego.

He might be.

The last time she'd seen him, she was sixteen, in her first year of med school. At Ronan's funeral. She'd spent twenty minutes talking to him. About what, she couldn't remember. That sad day was the first time he'd returned home since he stood in the front of the small chapel and called off his wedding…which had been supposed to start ten minutes before.

Ten years. Ten years that had been more than kind to him. He was tan. Broad-shouldered. And the last bits of boyhood had dropped away to chiseled features. Damn. Time had been *good.*

"Luca?"

His head snapped up, and Wren realized she'd spoken. At least that confirmed it was really him.

His dark beard was new. So was the hard look in his eyes as he tilted his head. The boy was cute. The man striking but not approachable. He waited a second, his gaze flicking across her. Did he recognize her?

"Do I know you?" He crossed his arms and leaned back in the chair.

Apparently not. That shouldn't sting. The last time he'd seen her she was sixteen with braces. A genius, according to all her professors and parents, but a girl lost in a world that only saw her for the mind she had. A child trapped in a world of adults.

Not accepted by the children her age or the adults impressed by her brain.

Ronan and Luca spent nearly every moment together before going to separate colleges. And they'd let his little sister, who never fit in anywhere, tag along on some of their adventures.

"Are you Luca McDonnell?" It was him. She knew it in her gut. But there was an air to him. A hardness she didn't remember.

"You called my name. Now you're questioning who you're talking to? Listen, if this is the birthday song from the hospital crew, I'm good. You don't have to do your little song and dance routine. Tell the owner of A Cappella Ambush you got me." Luca gestured to the stacks. "This is a library. Not really a good place for a birthday sing-along anyway."

"Are you hiding in the research center to avoid a birthday sing-along?" Wren walked up to the table and looked at the books covering it. Medical journals. Not a baseball book in sight. "Luca, why don't you want to be sung to?"

"My reasons are my own." He closed the book he'd been looking at, reached into his back pocket and pulled out a wallet. Then a hundred dollar bill. "You can tell whoever paid you that you found me, sang to me, and I was thoroughly embarrassed. That is the point of those, right?" He pushed the bill toward her, his eyes clearly telling her to get lost.

"I always thought it was for people to show you how much they cared about you?" Not that Wren really knew. Her parents didn't celebrate birthdays—

being born wasn't impressive. She hadn't gotten a birthday card or present since Ronan passed. "It's sweet that your friends want to celebrate you." Wren wasn't sure why she was arguing with him rather than telling him who she was. Maybe it was a futile hope that he'd realize she was not some singing telegram he was avoiding.

That he'd see her. Recognize her.

Luca rolled his bright green eyes to the ceiling. "Why are you just standing there? Do you want me to pay you more to go?" He pulled another hundred dollar bill from the wallet.

Holy hell!

If she was from the singing company, she'd have snatched the bills up and bid him goodbye. She'd done her fair share of odd jobs when her parents cut her off for daring to choose plastics instead of neurosurgery. The best discipline—the only one she was allowed if she wanted their praise and monetary support. She'd racked up monumental loans that she was only now getting a full grip on.

But that was not why she was here. It was almost like her brother had led her here. She grinned and laid Ronan's baseball card on the book in front of him.

Luca looked down and let out a breath. "How do you have—" His head snapped up. "Wren?"

"Don't need money." Not completely true, but that wasn't a topic for this interaction. "And not here to sing. Though, happy birthday." She frowned. "Wait, your birthday was two weeks ago."

Luca stood, and any hope she had that he'd reach out for a hug vanished as he crossed his arms. "It was. Why do you remember my birthday?"

There was a hint of anger in the question. A flash of something she didn't understand. They'd been close once. As close as the little sister of his best friend who was nearly a decade his junior could be.

When you put it that way, no wonder he's asking why you remember.

Words escaped her.

After a moment, he chuckled, a deep sound that carried in the quiet center. "Forgot." He tapped his head. "Your mind is basically a steel trap. Nothing gets out."

Wren rolled her eyes. She'd started kindergarten reading *Pride and Prejudice*. The teacher had marched her to the principal's office and demanded she test Wren to figure out where she belonged because it wasn't her room. It was an argument her parents had tried to make with the principal before she started. They'd not been pleased to hear the principal say she was sure her parents loved Wren and that she was bright, but every kid started in kindergarten.

Every kid in the town…except Wren.

She'd graduated high school at eleven. Started college at twelve and med school at sixteen. The steel trap mind. A gift…and a curse.

"Why would I forget your birthday? You're my friend." She paused. "Or you were. I guess we haven't seen each other in years."

Damn, this was awkward. Maybe she should have just walked past him, but she couldn't unring that bell.

Luca pulled at the back of his neck. "Your birthday is September 30." He grinned, his face finally relaxing. "I don't have a steel trap here—" he tapped his head again "—but I didn't forget. It's good to see you, Wren."

"It is nice of you to say that. Even if I'm not sure you really mean it." She laughed and held out her hand.

Luca looked at it, then shook his head. "Come on. We're old pals." He opened his arms, and she stepped into them.

Her body relaxed as he gripped her shoulders. She wrapped her arms around him. Her grip was too tight, but this was the first time in forever that someone had hugged her. Really hugged her.

She was apart from so many things. An oddity in conversations, where people much older than her looked at her accomplishments with jealousy or like she was some sort of zoo animal. Luca was a piece of home.

She squeezed him once more, then forced herself to step back, aware of the heat in her cheeks. "Do you live in San Diego?" The city was about as far as you could get from the small town they'd grown up in in Rhode Island.

"Yes." Luca pushed his hands into his pockets, pulling into himself.

"Wow. Don't give too much detail, Luca." Wren

bit her lip, then grabbed Ronan's card from the top of the book. "It was nice running into you."

"I feel like that's a lie." Luca looked at the books on the table, then at her.

She found a smile, trying to ignore the pinch of pain knowing it was clear he wasn't super excited to see her. "We're just a little rough around the edges discussion-wise. Ten years of lived experience between our younger selves and all." This wasn't a reunion any television show would emulate, but it was nice to know Luca was well. Even if he didn't want anyone to sing to him.

"Still the sunshiny optimist." Luca raised a brow. "The world hasn't sucked it out of you, yet?"

The world tried to steal her sunshine at least a few times a week. She simply refused to let it go. "I should get going."

"Bye, Wren." Luca nodded.

No way to stretch any conversation from that. Wren offered a final smile and tried to ignore the pain caused by the fact that he hadn't asked if she was just visiting or had moved here, or if she wanted to get together sometime soon.

He ran away from Lincoln and everyone in it. That includes me. What did I expect?

She turned on her heel, pitifully hoping he might call her back as she headed out of the stacks.

It wasn't until she was dropping the four fiction books the librarian recommended on her kitchen counter that she let the first tear fall. She was in a city where she knew exactly one person. And that man didn't want a connection with her.

Wren gave herself a little shake. She was starting at Sunshine Medical tomorrow. She'd meet people. Find friends. Build a life here.

The city was big enough. With any luck she'd never run into Luca again.

"If you want a pup cup before my shift starts, you need to get a move on, Hippo."

The beefy gray pittie mix tilted his head like he'd heard Luca, but then went right back to sniffing the spot on the sidewalk. The pup knew Luca wouldn't follow through with the threat.

Hippo might not know days of the week, but he knew that when Luca pulled the slip leash from the hook instead of the standard long blue leash, it meant it was treat day.

Luca waited a moment more, feeling a little bad that his best bud was going to be at day care for almost twelve hours today, then pulled on the leash and whistled.

Hippo snuffed, then moved beside Luca and started toward the coffee shop.

"I deserve that disgusted snuff, man." *Just not because I cut short your sniffing time.*

Luca had sat in his condo last night, Hippo in his lap, and thought of Wren.

Wren.

The girl he'd known had transformed into a stunning woman. One he'd not-so-subtly checked out:

her long hair pulled into a loose braid, her dark chocolate eyes, the button nose. It had taken him a moment to react, telling her to get lost; because he thought she was part of the sing-along crew the hospital peds unit hired. The one trying so hard to make sure he got the "gift" the peds department purchased.

Then he'd realized who she was. He'd been checking out his late best friend's little sister. Hell, he'd had to cross his arms to keep from reaching out to her. Then he'd hugged her anyway….and held on way too long. She'd been the one to end the hug. He'd made sure the conversation didn't drag on after that.

Rude. I was rude.

There was no sugarcoating it. Wren was Ronan's little sister; Luca owed it to him to find a way to make amends. So he'd spent far too long looking for her online last night.

He'd deleted all his social media apps from his phone a while ago. The only contacts who reached out were exes in search of money. Or family, also in search of money. A fact that was clear when he logged back in and found more than sixty direct messages from his mother and father. Both had his phone number. Both could call to check on him. Say hi.

He didn't know why social media was the one place the people who were supposed to love him reached out. Always with the same ask for more money.

If they acted like they cared about him at all, he'd cave and send what they asked. But they couldn't even ask basic *how are you* questions. Or tell him they missed him. Apologize for the giant fight they'd had the last time they'd talked.

Because they don't miss me.

That was a tough lesson to learn.

Still he'd logged back into all the apps last night to see if he could locate her. Then he'd created a few dummy accounts on apps he heard about at the hospital. Wren wasn't on the one most of the young nurses and doctors discussed, and she wasn't on the networking site the newest physical therapist, Therese Cameron, suggested he join if he wanted to advance his career.

No one believed him when he said he had no interest in making a career change. He'd worked at Sunrise Medical since graduating from physical therapy school. Still held the same position as staff doctor of physical therapy, DPT in medical jargon.

He never put in for a promotion. Never tried to move to another place.

After all, it wasn't like he needed the money. A fact none of his colleagues knew. After his ex-fiancée, Madeline, walked out on him, he'd made sure to never tell the women he dated about his financial situation.

Though they all eventually found out. Then the demands started. He had the same issue with friends.

Once upon a time he'd been the friend people

called to tell good news and bad. The friend who took you to the bar when your significant other cheated. The friend who listened when the world was upside down and celebrated when you were on top of the world.

After people found out about his worth, he became the bank. No more silly texts with gifs and inside jokes. No more happy hour trips to share a bucket of beer. Nope.

Hell, when he'd told one of his friends about Madeline's confession that she didn't love him, the friend had joked that Luca could buy love. The man got upset when Luca said it wasn't funny. His friend made it clear that he thought it was dumb that Luca was so upset when he had enough money not to worry about anything. *Take yourself on vacation. Buy a new sports car.*

Like things could make up for finding out the woman you loved saw you as a checkbook.

He'd quickly figured out that no one thought he could have problems because he had money. It didn't take long for him to become the invisible friend… until someone needed a loan, or more accurately, a gift.

The only person who hadn't cared about his unexpected windfall was Ronan. His best friend. The brother of the woman he'd treated so poorly yesterday.

If his friend had seen him, Luca would have gotten a smack on the back of the head. And he'd have earned it.

He owed Wren an apology but had no idea how to find her. She'd been in her first year of med school at Ronan's funeral. Had she completed it? Of course she had. Probably with honors. Wren was a certified genius.

What was her specialty? Was she working at Sunrise? Or in town for a medical conference?

All questions I could, and should, have asked yesterday.

Hippo let out a squeal. The squat pittie mix hardly ever barked. He chirped. It was a weird, solely Hippo thing.

"Yes, we're almost there." Luca grinned as the dog started his happy dance, his routine every time they stepped onto the block for the Cupcake Café. In the morning, it had coffee and breakfast. At ten, it switched to coffee and cupcakes.

The door of the café opened, and Hippo let out a soft "ahroo!"

The woman holding the door turned, and Luca's breath caught. It was like he'd willed her into being. "Wren."

"Luca." Wren looked at the door and let go. Then reached for it again. "Did you need this? Wait—" Her eyes darted to Hippo, and she released the door again. His appearance clearly frazzled her. At least he wasn't the only one out of sorts. "And who is this?"

Hippo danced and nosed toward the door of the cafe. "Hippo. Who needs his pup cup. Although *need* is probably an overstatement."

He headed to the light pole where he always tied Hippo before he slipped into the bakery. He ordered online, so it never took more than a moment.

"I can hold him. If you want. And if you think he'll let me." Wren bent and rubbed Hippo's head.

A hint of chamomile wafted through Luca's senses, and he started to lean a little closer.

Ronan's sister. Ronan's sister.

The dog sighed and laid his head against her knee. For just an instant, Luca was jealous of his dog.

Ronan's sister.

He shouldn't need the reminder. The pink bandana he'd let the dog choose fell across Wren's knee. *Choose* was a relative statement with Hippo, but Luca always held up two bandannas for the chunkster to select from. The dog refused to go anywhere without one, and the collection he'd amassed was more than over the top.

Mentally, Luca shook himself. He needed to get moving, both because he had to get to work and because his brain was far too focused on the way Wren's pencil skirt hugged her hips. "The only thing he loves more than pup cups is attention. If you don't mind—"

"I don't." Wren held out her free hand for the leash. "I have to have the leash if I'm going to pet you."

Luca slipped the leash around her wrist, careful to make sure his fingers didn't brush her delicate-looking skin, then started for the door, very aware that neither Hippo or Wren were paying him any attention. At least he'd get a chance to apologize. He grabbed the order and headed right back out the door.

"See, no time at all." He bent and held out the pup cup.

And Hippo ignored him.

"Hippo?" Luca waved the whipped cream mini cup in front of the dog. Hippo had tippy-tapped down the sidewalk, knowing what was coming. And nothing! He just kept soaking in Wren's attention.

"Maybe if I stood, he might be more interested in what you got him." Wren kissed the top of Hippo's head and then stood. "It was nice to meet you, Hippo." She turned to Luca but didn't say anything.

Like I can blame her.

"Need to get him to day care before my shift," Luca began. That was not what he was supposed to say, but his brain seemed to give up its ability to make words around her. He felt his stomach drop as Wren simply nodded. She turned and started walking the opposite way he needed to go.

"Wren!" His call was too loud. It wasn't like she'd taken more than a step.

She lifted her coffee to her lips and looked at him over the lid.

"Sorry I wasn't more welcoming yesterday. I was rude. It was undeserved." Luca crumpled the very empty pup cup that Hippo had made quick work of and threw it in the trash can. "Just…sorry."

"I'm the one that sneaked up on you, Luca. No apology needed." She beamed.

Sunshine seemed to bend around her. Beauty and brains. The complete package. And his best friend's little sister.

Your dead best friend's little sister.

The definition of forbidden.

"It was good to see you. Not a lie." He paused as the next words he should utter stuck in his throat. *Ask why she's here. How long she's staying. Her phone number.*

But none of those questions made it from his brain to his lips. He'd cut off everyone from his hometown after Madeline's announcement in the bridal suite the day of their wedding. Only Ronan had been allowed to stay in his life.

And he was gone, too.

Wren was a tie to that old life. A link to the man Luca had been. The man he'd buried when he heard his fiancée confess to her maid of honor that she wasn't really in love with him. But she'd found out that he had inherited his aunt's estate…and the millions she'd hidden from his family.

His aunt's final letter to Luca had told him she thought the money was cursed and hoped it brought him more joy than it did her. He'd laughed at the line, half wondering if his aunt, so sharp, had lost it in her final days without him knowing. Then he heard Madeline explain her plan to stick it out, at least for a year or two…because there was no prenup.

The worst part was knowing he should have picked up on it. She was distant for weeks before the wedding. Excited at the idea of the party, the white dress, but not their life together. He'd chalked his concerns up to cold feet. Ignoring the tiny voice inside his head screaming *danger*.

Then there were the not-so-subtle hints that they needed to make the most out of their first years together. When he'd reminded her that he was finishing residency, she'd pointed out that she could find someone to travel with her. Not bummed at all that her future husband couldn't accompany her on the trips she planned.

She'd never pointed out that with all the money he had, they could both quit their jobs… Something she did the day after he told her about his inheritance.

The red flags were there. He just hadn't wanted to see them.

Curse: 1. Luca: 0.

That was not the only time the curse had crossed his path. Once Luca had learned he was only wanted for the funds he brought, he'd clammed up, just like his aunt. Still, you always remembered the one who hurt you first.

Wren waited a minute longer, the silence hovering loudly between them. Then she raised her coffee cup. "Have a good morning, Luca."

This time when she turned to walk away, he didn't try to stop her.

He watched her round the corner. Her pencil

skirt, bright yellow button-down shirt and two-inch pumps hardly indicated she was heading to a hospital. Most likely in town for a conference.

He'd bought a condo near the San Diego Convention Center because it was available and the area was busy. Technically, he'd bought the building, but the location was the reason. The area was easy to get lost in. The rentals were mostly tech bros and tired medical professionals. On the streets, it was tourists he ran past most days.

Since he wasn't interested in networking, he never looked to see if there was anything of interest at the convention center. Maybe he'd check the schedule later. See what was in town. If there were any times in the schedule when Wren might be on a break.

To do what?

He'd been downright rude in the library. And awkward as hell this morning. A third meeting to make sure she knew he wasn't interested in rekindling any relationship from his past was hardly necessary.

Luca shook his head and whistled for Hippo to follow. "Time to get you to day care and me to the hospital."

Hippo snuffled and walked beside him.

"At least you never tire of me." He rubbed the dog's head and let out a sigh.

The millions his aunt left him were supposed to make his life easier. And, in many ways, they had. He'd graduated college and physical therapy school with no debt. A feat few of his classmates could boast of. He owned a building in a city most only dreamed of moving to.

But as soon as people found out, they looked at him different. Madeline had simply been the first.

There were three other partners who'd seen him as a ticket to freedom rather than a loved one, once they discovered his fortune. Three partners he'd nearly convinced himself would be different.

And they never were.

Then there was Ronan. The only one he'd had to pester into letting him help. Ronan's parents had refused to help him get a car. Refused to help him with anything. So Luca cosigned on the loan for the car Ronan bought. He'd have bought him a new car, but Ronan had barely wanted the signature.

If Luca had pushed him into a new car, would things have been different? A bigger vehicle, one that might have stood a chance when it was T-boned by a huge truck? He'd never know.

Curse: infinity. Luca: 0.

He had Hippo and the career he wanted. Luca didn't need anything else.

Most days he believed it.

CHAPTER TWO

ORIENTATION DAY. HER LEAST favorite day in a new hospital. Wren had hoped the hospital wouldn't make a big deal about her arrival. Yes, she was the youngest board-certified plastic surgeon in the country. And she had helped develop a new debridement technique that gave patients a better chance of full recovery of movement in their limbs following a third degree burn. But she was also just another new hire starting this month.

Except, unlike others starting today, she was currently being shown around the facility not by human resources, like the rest of the new hires, but by Dr. Seth Graham, one of the top plastic surgeons in the city, who she was certain had other things to do.

"This is maternity." Dr. Graham pointed to a wing with pastel colors and a locked entrance. "You have to scan to get in, and all the babies have coded bands around their ankles to make sure they don't leave."

Wren nodded. It was a security measure most hospitals had in place to prevent kidnapping. Not something parents wanted to think about, but there had been cases.

"And this…" Seth beamed as they rounded a corner "…is physical therapy."

"You spend a lot of time in physio?" Many physio patients would rotate down here following their surgeries, but there wasn't much need for their surgeon to check in on them beyond the notes in their chart. Though she had made it a habit to stop in at least a few times when her patients were transitioning to PT.

"Seth." A white woman grinned at the surgeon as they stepped into the surprisingly quiet physio room.

"Dr. Freson, this is my fiancée, Therese. Dr. Freson is the new plastics specialist everyone has been so excited to meet."

Wren held out a hand. "Please call me Wren. It's nice to meet you, Therese."

"Nice to meet you, too. I bet you're loving this walk around, right?" The woman smiled. "I started not that long ago. First days are nerve-racking."

"Yes. Yes, they are."

Seth looked around the room, raising an eyebrow. "No patients?"

"Nope." Therese blew out a breath. "Both my morning patients refused to come to therapy today." She looked at the empty stations. "Frustrating. This is why I prefer working with peds. The kids always want to give it a go."

Adults had the right to say no to treatment. The right to ignore the doctor's orders, even though it would set their progress back. It was a frustrating but not infrequent occurrence.

"Physical therapy is hard." Wren had heard more

than one patient refer to physio as torture. It wasn't, but often the road to health was paved with pain.

Therese nodded. "Where are you heading to next?"

"You are our last stop." Seth smiled warmly at Therese. "Saved the best for last. And we got lucky because McSteamy isn't here."

"McSteamy?" Wren repeated. She watched the hint of color rise on Seth's neck.

"I shouldn't call him that," he said.

Therese shrugged. "She's going to hear his nickname soon anyway."

"Is there a hot doc I'm supposed to be warned off?" Wren had never had any interest in dating her colleagues. Besides, when you were so much younger than your colleagues and classmates, it didn't allow for much romantic socializing. Though she was twenty-six now, so opportunities might arise.

Not that I'd have any idea what to do with a hot doc.

She'd gone on exactly three dates—ever. Each a spectacular failure. So she was a twenty-six old virgin with no dating experience. What a catch.

"He is conventionally attractive, but that's not the reason for the nickname. He's—"

"A hothead. Annoying. And short with everyone." Luca's words filled the space behind her as he stepped into the physio room.

No. No. There was no way he was here. Yet, "Mc-

Steamy" fit the man she'd met in the library…and this morning. Hot. Man of few words.

She watched him walk past her, his gaze firmly planted on the tablet chart in his hands. "Mr. McDaniels had therapy in his room. He promises to come here tomorrow."

Luca walked over to the computer station and started typing notes—presumably into a chart. No hello, no surprise that she was the new surgeon on staff…which if she was fair was probably because he hadn't bothered to look at her at all.

"He promised me the same yesterday." Therese shook her head. "On good days, this place is loud and noisy. And some days…" She gestured to the room. "Hopefully the afternoon cases will be better."

Luca made a short sound under his breath but didn't add any commentary.

"Luca." Seth's voice was level, but she heard the stern surgeon voice used to get attention. "I apologize for discussing your nickname with the new surgeon."

"Everyone knows it. Not a secret." He still didn't look up from the monitor.

"This is the new burn specialist. I was tasked to show her around." Seth waited a minute, but when Luca didn't respond, he turned to Wren. "Dr. Freson, are you—"

"Freson?" Now Luca's head popped up.

If Seth was surprised by the reaction, he didn't show it.

Luca's gaze met hers, his eyes wide. He didn't say anything for several seconds. Finally, he cleared his throat. "Freson like the Link-Freson technique?"

He was covering. Using her achievement to push away any chance to show they knew each other.

Fine. Two could play that game.

"Yes, I am Dr. Freson from that technique." Her face heated. Why did she always have that reaction when someone brought up her greatest achievement? She and Dr. Sonja Link had spent more than one late night studying in the library as interns. Going over burn images, horrid images, and spitballing new ideas. Not that they'd expected it to become more than shop talk. Until one night they struck gold.

Her male colleagues would never blush over such a discovery. It made her seem young and inexperienced. She was young…but not inexperienced.

"Sonja, Dr. Link, is still at the hospital in New York where we developed it."

"Why are you here? A big hospital in New York is most people's dream." Luca tilted his head, his jade gaze pinning her down.

He still hadn't acknowledged that he knew her. That she'd spent a few minutes holding his dog for him this morning. He was gruff and unapproachable. The exact opposite of the young man she'd known.

"Memorial General in New York City, like this one, is a teaching hospital. Sonja stayed there, and I came here. We can teach more plastics and burn specialists the technique. Aid in healing." Wren shrugged. "I am here because we drew straws."

"Was Sunrise the short-end straw?" Therese wasn't frowning, but there was tension in her shoulders.

"No." Wren turned her attention to Therese. "I drew the long straw, which meant I got to choose. I was ready to leave New York City."

She'd started at Memorial as a resident. A very young, inexperienced resident. She was at the top of her field. But there were some there who would only ever see the resident who was too young to drink on their first day in scrubs. A genius physician, with very little life experience.

Wren wanted, needed, a new start. Somewhere people had a chance to see her for her. That didn't mean it was easy to leave Sonja behind.

"Sonja will be the head of plastics at Memorial in a few years, I have no doubt. Plus, her girlfriend and family are in the area. I was probably always the one coming out here, but no, Sunrise was my choice. Doesn't mean starting here isn't nerve-racking. Hope that's okay." She glanced at Therese, hoping the physical therapist knew she was where she wanted to be.

"One can be thrilled and terrified at the same time." Therese's gaze shot to Seth. His look was so full of love that Wren felt like she'd stepped into a private conversation.

She looked toward Luca; his gaze was rooted to

hers. But the friendly face she'd hoped to find was absent.

It was fine.

He didn't want a connection to his past. In many ways she didn't, either. They were strangers. A decade between them and their younger selves.

Fine!

"I wasn't going to come." Patrick McDaniels gripped the railing and started to slowly climb the four steps the physical therapy room had to simulate climbing much larger stairs.

Luca nodded. The man was only sixty-five. If he worked hard, there was no reason he couldn't return to the life he'd had before the car accident that broke his left leg and fractured his pelvis last month. The road was long, and he probably hadn't undergone his last surgery, but pushing through physical therapy was the only way to get back to that—no matter how much it hurt.

"Wasn't gonna come." Patrick puffed as he made it up the third step.

If that was the mantra he needed to push himself through, fine. Therese was the nice physio—or at least nicer than Luca. The woman still very much pushed her patients. He was the one who firm. Never mean but straightforward. Some patients needed that.

Patrick started making his way down the stairs and let out a breath. "I blame Dr. Freson." He glared at the stairs as he hit the bottom step.

"You need to go up again." Luca wasn't sure why a patient who should have no interaction with Wren was blaming her for coming to physical therapy.

"I know!" He let more than one curse word out under his breath, then pushed himself up the first step. "Dr. Freson said she'd get me an ice cream if I came down here. This is not worth ice cream." He glared at Luca.

Luca had spent the last two days hearing all about Dr. Freson. Wren had started her shift the day after the horrid introduction in this room. Not that they'd needed an introduction. Though no one would have known it from his reaction.

He'd been focused on three patients who'd refused treatment, pissed and glaring at their charts on the tablet looking for some reason the entire morning group would tell him to pound sand. Luca convinced two of three to do a few workouts in their rooms, but both had given up after less than five minutes.

He hadn't even realized there was anyone with Seth and Therese. Ever since those two had gotten engaged, it wasn't surprising to find Seth spending his limited free time saying hi to Therese. He'd heard them jabbering about the nickname a nurse gave him years ago. It didn't bother him. Luca was a loner.

By the time he'd realized that Wren was there and connected her to the debridement technique, his brain had lost most of its ability to think clearly.

The Link-Freson technique had revolutionized

burn care. And yet she'd blushed when he mentioned it.

If almost anyone else had codeveloped that, it would be off their tongue immediately after saying their name. As it should be, honestly. But Wren would not have brought it up if he hadn't.

More than one exhausted resident had boasted how nice it was to have her at the hospital while waiting in line at the cafeteria. How caring and approachable she was.

It was not making it easy to drive her from his mind.

"Let her talk me into this for ice cream." Patrick made it to the top step again and started his descent. "Not even my doctor."

"Then how did she convince you to come to physical therapy?" Patrick McDaniel was the first person he'd heard complain about Wren. Everyone was quick to talk about how sunny she was. How happy. Quick to smile. A good listener. And so down to earth.

In other words, perfect.

Patrick hit the bottom step and started back up without Luca having to goad him. A good sign.

"My roommate needs reconstructive work on his hand. I was grumbling that he got ice cream, and Micah said I didn't deserve any since I was just loafing." Patrick rolled his eyes, but there was color along his neck that indicated he was embarrassed by the assessment.

Maybe that would motivate him.

"Dr. Freson said she'd get me ice cream if you said I'd come to the room and done all my exercises."

"All your exercises?"

His patient hit the top step and looked back at him. "Yes. But this is the last of the exercises you listed when I got here. I expect you to tell Dr. Freson I earned that ice cream."

A deal was a deal. "I will relay the message in the chart." Luca doubted he'd see Wren. The woman had no reason to be in the physical therapy room. No reason to seek him out. He'd made sure of that.

Patrick finished up his exercise and accepted the water cup Luca offered.

"You did good work here today."

"I know." Patrick raised his arms. "All for a cup of vanilla ice cream."

There was something in the way he said it. "You don't like vanilla?" Weird to work for something you didn't want, but Luca would take it.

Patrick finished his water and passed it back. "It's fine. I mean vanilla is vanilla, and it's not like I can get cherry chip in the hospital." He closed his eyes. "I am tired."

Luca nodded. "You worked hard, and your stamina is not what it was. You have to work back up to it. I know it hurts to come here, but it's the only way you'll get to feel like yourself again."

"I hate you. And I hate this." Patrick swallowed as he pinched his eyes closed. The man was close to tears, and Luca knew he wanted to be alone while he went through the emotions racing through him.

"Let's get you back to your room." As a physical therapist, he was used to being his patients' least favorite person. He saw them at their lowest, weakest point. He'd accept the hate if it made them better.

After dropping Patrick off, Luca headed to the nurses' station to give a short report and find out if they knew where he might find a pint of cherry chip ice cream. Patrick had earned it.

As soon as he headed toward the elevator, he got a tingle on the back of his neck. He looked back at the nurses' station. One of them was on the phone and had too big a smile.

Luca waited for the elevator to open and stepped inside. But he didn't hit the button for the second floor where the physical therapy suite was. He smiled as the elevator started heading up instead of down. He was not going to get caught by the singing telegram. Not today.

The door opened on the sixth floor. Luca stepped out and headed for the stairwell. He raced down the steps and nearly ran into Wren on her way up.

"Dr. McDonnell." Wren put her hand on his shoulder to steady herself and lightning shot through his body.

A silly schoolboy reaction to a gorgeous woman. A woman completely off-limits to him, even if he was interested in dating.

"I thought you were on a first-name basis with everyone." Luca pulled back, far too aware of the chamomile scent wafting from her hair and the tilt of her lips as she frowned.

Wren stepped around him. "You are clearly in a rush."

"Not really. Just avoiding a singing telegram. It was clear when I dropped Patrick McDaniel off the nurses were giving a heads-up to someone that I was heading down. They aren't allowed in patient spaces. I'll slip into the back of the physio room and wait them out."

Wren rolled her eyes. "You'd think people who call you McSteamy would figure out you don't want this."

Luca leaned against the stairwell wall. "This is the first year they've tried to get me. I guess one of the nurses said it wasn't fair that I was left out." This would be the last year they attempted it, he was certain of that. "No doubt they regret it now. McSteamy is no fun after all."

He started to move around her, but she put her hand on his shoulder. The touch lasted less than a second, but it was enough to send his heart rate up.

"You may have them fooled, but I know the truth. You're still just a giant softie."

Once upon a time, a gorgeous, intelligent woman putting her hands on him and looking at him with soft brown eyes would have brought him to his knees.

Who was he kidding? Wren was causing that exact reaction.

"The nickname is dumb, but don't romanticize

me. I do not make friends. I do not date." He leaned a little closer, to make a point, not because he was drawn to her. "And I am a grade A asshole."

"A grade A asshole with a chunky dog named Hippo. Nope."

Luca crossed his arms and forced himself to retreat. "Lots of assholes have dogs."

"Sure. But true assholes don't have bandanna-wearing, pup-cup-craving, tippy-toe-dancing babies." She started up the steps but turned on the next landing. "Don't worry, McSteamy, I won't spill your secret." She gave a quick wink and was off.

CHAPTER THREE

LUCA ROLLED HIS SHOULDERS, trying to loosen the pinch between his shoulder blades. He'd slept wrong. Or, more accurate, hadn't been able to sleep given the constant tossing and turning he'd done while trying to drive thoughts of Wren from his mind. Since running into each other at the library, she stormed into his dreams every time he'd drifted off.

Stormed.

Luca laughed at the thought. Wren didn't storm anywhere. She entered, gracefully, fully in control of every room. And in his dreams, she was entering wearing far less clothing.

Ronan's little sister.

Why was the one person on this planet who was firmly off-limits the one he couldn't drive from his thoughts? Ronan was his best friend. The only person from his old life who'd only wanted just his friendship. The only one who'd kept their relationship exactly the same after his aunt's legacy. Lucas owed it to him to find a way to banish the thoughts.

"You're frowning so hard the whole coffee shop is afraid to step over here." Wren grinned as she hit her hip against his. "Smile."

"Very cute, Wren." He looked over the crowd, and a tingle shot down his back. He needed his coffee…and the orders were moving slowly. Too slowly. The Sunrise to Sunset Café catered to the hospital staff and visitors who wanted to be with their loved ones. They were efficient. This was unusual.

Something he might have noticed, if he hadn't been thinking about the beauty before him now.

"I am very cute." She tilted her head. "Smile. You remember how, right?"

Luca furrowed his brow and looked toward the area where the baristas were dropping orders. "I don't need to smile."

Wren looked at her feet, then back at him, her dark gaze mesmerizing. "You're right. You don't need to. It was rude of me to tell you to."

"Wren."

"Are you okay?" She put a hand on his arm.

The connection burned. Where was his damn coffee? He'd already paid, so there was no reason to just walk away.

"I'm fine." He looked around her. Was she trying to keep him here? It had taken her exactly twenty-four hours to make everyone in the hospital her friend. At this rate, most of the facility would do anything she asked. At least that was the way it seemed.

The woman was the talk of the hospital. And not because she was a legit genius. Everyone was talking about how personable she was. How kind. How good with patients.

"Ronan used to joke that when his girlfriend said

she was fine, it meant danger. I wonder if it means the same for you?"

Ronan. Girlfriend.

The connection to his past. Wren was that connection. She was a colleague. But rather than making sure a singing telegram didn't go to waste, she was checking on him.

When was the last time that happened?

"I'm just anxious because my coffee is delayed. Considering it's just a basic coffee, I wouldn't have thought it would take this much time, but…" He looked at the counter and closed his eyes. "I'm being trapped."

He moved to step around her, but Wren held up her hand. "Wait."

He opened his mouth, but before any words came out, the song started. "Happy birthday to you…"

The singing group was all smiles. The people around the coffee corner were clapping and singing along. If it wasn't for Wren, he'd have darted out before it started. He'd been so absorbed by her that he missed all the signs gathering around him. Too late to do anything about it now.

He waited for them to finish, nodded his head to the group who looked more than a little relieved to have gotten the job done, then looked at the barista. "My coffee finally done?"

"Oh, I have to get it made. Sorry. We just—"

Luca waved them off. "Just forget it. Nice job trapping me, Wren. No doubt that will be the talk of at least a few nurses' stations today. You accomplished what they couldn't." *Because I let you.*

There was no point waiting for her response. He had patients and needed to get going. He raised a hand to the singers and headed for the physical therapy room.

They had gotten him. Fair and square. *All because I can't get my best friend's little sister out of my head.* That ended now.

"Luca! Luca!" The call followed him down the hall.

"You won, Wren. Nice job." He spun and nearly knocked the two coffees out of her hands.

"Yours." She pressed it toward him. "You already paid for it, and the barista was in tears. I told her I was the one who called the peds floor to let them know where you were, so she didn't need to feel bad for letting them know, too."

"So you *did* rat me out?" He'd suspected that. Hated that he'd missed the warning signals, but somehow it still hurt to know that she'd helped with something he so clearly didn't want.

Not like it's the first time I didn't pick up clear signals.

"No. I didn't actually call peds." She shook her head. "But Maggie was so upset, and this way she doesn't have to worry over it."

Luca took a sip of his coffee. "It wasn't you?" His stomach unclenched, and his soul felt like it took a breath. He hadn't misread Wren.

"No. Though I still don't understand the reason

you hate the birthday sing-along." Wren rolled her eyes before looking over her shoulder. "They did it because they thought it was nice, and despite the aura you put off, you are good with patients. Peds didn't want you left out."

The lid of his coffee cup popped. Clearly, he'd squeezed more than a little too hard. He bent down, grabbed it and blew out a breath as he looked at Wren. "You were probably too young to remember, but my parents announced their divorce on my tenth birthday." He shook his head. "It did not make me a huge fan of celebrating it."

After that nightmare, every birthday was a one-upmanship contest, his parents only caring about him when they could use him to hurt the other. His parents were takers, two people unable to see other people for anything more than what they could gain from them. A lesson it had taken him far too long to learn.

Wren's face lost all its color. "I was a newborn at that party, assuming my parents even brought me. I didn't know."

"Yeah, well, the only other person that would re-member was Ronan, and he…" Luca was done with this conversation. "Thanks for the coffee. I have pa-tients to see, and I'm sure you do, too."

"Do you want me to let them know? Or are you counting on this display of aggressive avoidance getting you out of celebrating next year?"

He didn't have time for this discussion. "There is no way they will get me a birthday song next year.

Please. I know they tried to get a refund, but the owner of the company stood his ground. Said that he'd never not provided a perfect service." It was ridiculous. Jessica, one of the charge nurses working on the peds floor, had apologized repeatedly. They'd already found another company for the next go-round.

Wren looked at her watch. This conversation was drawing to an end. Something he was now loath to have happen. He needed to get himself in check.

"They won't do the song, but if you are anti-celebration, letting them know so there isn't a birthday cake or something small to recognize you next year isn't a terrible idea." Wren shrugged. "Anyway, if you want me quietly let them know, you know where I work. Always happy to help."

"How the hell do you do this?" The words escaped, and he wanted to scream at himself. *McSteamy never talks* was a complaint he'd heard more than once from one colleague to another. Yet somehow his tongue loosened around Wren without fail. And not in a good way.

"Do what?"

"Act all bubbly? Put out this vibe of sunshine when you know the world is horrid."

Wren straightened her shoulders. "It is hardly horrid."

"Your brother died right as his dreams were coming true." He pulled a hand across his face. "That was over the line."

"Saying it was over the line is not an apology."

Wren raised her chin. The look in her eyes touched his core. It was pure strength.

This was a woman who'd graduated high school, college and med school with people ten years her senior. The woman who'd created a new technique to change lives and moved across the country on her own.

"I apologize."

She nodded, and this time it was Wren turning on her heel and walking away.

"I hate this." Lena Stevens looked away as Wren pulled the dressings from her hand. The burns were healing nicely. That did not mean her hand looked anything like it had before her ex-boyfriend doused her arm in lighter fluid and lit a match.

"It's looking good, Lena." Wren looked at the damaged fingers. "I know it hurts, but have you met with the physical therapists?"

It was a question Wren knew the answer to. Lena had refused to meet with Therese yesterday and Luca the day before. According to the nurses, she'd gotten out of bed to use the facilities but nothing else. Mental health had done an evaluation and added antidepressants to the medicinal cocktail she received. But it would be weeks before the SSRIs took full effect.

Lena let out a puff of air. Not much of an answer.

"It's important to start doing small movements to get your range of motion back. The wound—"

"Looks good. I know. Everyone says it's healing.

It looks so much better than we thought. Oh, Lena, don't you know how lucky you are." Lena pinched her eyes closed, but it didn't stop the tears leaking down her face. "Lucky. Lucky. I hate that stupid word. I hate it."

Well, she was talking, and Wren was going to take every advantage. Anger was a fantastic motivator.

"None of this is lucky. And my hand does not look good. It looks monstrous. But hey, Donald only destroyed my hand. The fire could have been so much worse."

Her tone let Wren know she was mimicking someone. Whether it was a nurse or family, Wren didn't know.

There was truth in the statement, though. The incident occurred two weeks before Wren started at Sunrise. From what she'd heard, if Lena hadn't had a fire blanket nearby because of her artwork, it would have been much worse. That did not mean it was helpful information right now.

"My hand. My art." She bit her lip so hard Wren worried she was tasting blood.

Wren sat on the edge of the bed. "I am not going to lie to you, your hand will never look the same." She gently lifted Lena's injured hand. "The skin graft is adjusting well. I fully believe that you will get full range of motion back in your fingers and hand."

"He took the thing I loved most. He stole my primary means of making money. My way of making joy." Lena moved her hand, slowly, but she was looking at it. This was her body; the body part that was the driving force of her livelihood.

Wren had heard so many platitudes growing up.

They're just jealous of you.

You'll make friends when you're older.

Your mind is a gift, don't waste it.

Not a single one made the situation better. She was a genius. That was what people saw. What people cared about. That life experience meant she never sugarcoated the news she had to deliver to her patients. "I mean it, Lena. Your fingers will regain the same range of motion in time. It won't be easy, but it can be accomplished."

"So my art will be the same." Lena looked at her with a flicker of hope.

"I doubt it." Wren let out a sigh. "You've gone through a life-changing event. It changed you. And I suspect your art will change because of that. But your hand will accomplish what you want it to."

"I didn't want the change." More tears streamed down Lena's cheeks.

Wren understood that. Her life had a few breaking points but nothing as sizable as the chasm that opened at Ronan's funeral. Before that fateful day, her mind had protected her.

Despite knowing what had happened, part of Wren believed she'd wake from the nightmare. Ronan would send a silly meme when she texted him the horrid dream. But seeing his urn at the funeral home was the second it became truly real, and she changed. Not intentionally. And not because she wanted to.

There was a before. And there was after. A person was not the same when they stepped into the after.

"I know you didn't want this. It is not fair. In fact, it is downright shitty."

Lena's mouth widened at the curse, but her eyes brightened. "Yes. It is."

Naming it, calling the change out helped Wren. She'd stood in the cemetery when everyone was gone and screamed at the stone. Cursed the world, the fates, the universe. All of it. Grief stayed with you. A constant that never really faded. Your life grew bigger around it but never vanquished it. However, you couldn't let it rule you.

"You can't let him win, Lena. You have a gift. He only steals that gift from you if *you* let him."

Lena looked at her arm, but she didn't cringe this time. "You think I can get the full range of motion back? That I will be able to hold a fine tip paintbrush and create the softest strokes?"

"I do." Wren stated it firmly. There was a long road ahead, but Lena's injuries would not stop her from creating. "It won't be tomorrow. Or even next week, but with time and physical therapy, you will get everything back."

"Did someone say physical therapy?" Luca stepped into the room. His gaze went directly to Wren, and she suspected he'd heard at least part of the conversation.

Lena was still looking at her hand. "Full range of motion." She smiled and looked at Luca. "I want my full range of motion. I want to paint. I need to paint. Yeah. I'm ready for physical therapy."

There was a small twitch in his jaw, but he smiled at Lena. "Music to my ears." Luca nodded to Wren. "Why don't you stay a moment, Dr. Freson? We're going to start with some exercises here. Things you can do on your own without me," he told Lena.

Wren stepped around Luca. She wasn't sure why he wanted her in the room, and after their argument this morning, she'd plotted different pathways to limit her chances of seeing him.

"Please stay a minute, Dr. Freson. Please." Wren had not considered leaving, but Lena's plea would have stalled her feet if she had.

"Of course."

Luca pulled a soft ball from the small container all the physios carried around with them. Little tools they could use in the rooms and leave behind for patients.

"Step one is squeezing this ball." He passed the ball to Lena.

She looked at it. "This shouldn't be hard."

Luca didn't correct her. This was a humbling lesson many patients had to learn. You started at least two steps behind where you thought you would.

Lena started squeeze it, and though she was trying to keep her face clear, it was obvious this was rougher than she expected.

"It's a squishy ball." She made the comment to herself, but Luca nodded.

"It is. And if you're in here watching TV or reading or just lying here, squeeze it several times until you're sore but not hurting. Hurting will not do you any good. In fact, it will set you back. Once you are able to do it for three minutes, I'll shift you to this." He pulled another ball from his container.

"Doesn't look much different." Lena glared at the ball in her hand, but she forced her hand to close around it two more times. "Full range of motion. Full range of motion."

If that was the mantra that kept her going, Wren was fine with it. But the look in Luca's eyes made her uneasy.

"I am going to see another patient. Good work, Lena." She ducked out before Luca or Lena could say anything else.

CHAPTER FOUR

WREN'S FEET POUNDED on the treadmill. She'd planned to do at least five miles outside, but the rain and not really knowing her surroundings had forced her to the gym in the basement of her new building.

The building catered to young tech bros and a couple of tired surgeons. The manager had insisted on showing her a massive apartment on an upper floor that was empty. The rent for the year would have run her close to a million dollars. As if she could afford that.

She was in a one-bedroom. The manager had not hidden her frustration at her inability to upsell Wren to a two-bedroom. But what did she need two bedrooms for? Plus, she was still making payments on student loans that would stay with her for at least another ten years. Med school was not cheap. And she'd even had a few scholarships and help from her parents—at least for the first year.

Wren spent the first weekend unpacking and trying to figure out the decorating scheme she wanted. She'd chosen this apartment because the lease agreement stated that as long as she didn't change the structure, she could do whatever she wanted.

As soon as she figured out what that was. Today, though, she was checking out the gym.

At least the tech bros the manager had bragged about weren't around. Likely they had expensive gym equipment in the four bedroom apartments they rented or memberships to an upscale gym.

Wren started running in college. Though considering she'd started at twelve, one could consider it a childhood activity. It was freeing. Headphones, trails, nothing and nobody to compare herself to.

That was not true of all runners. She'd quit two running groups because they were competing for most miles or some other metric. This was the one thing she never measured.

The gym door opened, but she didn't turn around. She was here to work out. There were three treadmills, and she saw the man start the one next to her. Wren rolled her eyes but didn't turn her head.

Luckily, despite choosing the machine next to her, the man never initiated conversation. He'd sped up his machine and kept a solid pace beside her. That might be intentional, but she still had at least two miles to go, and if he insisted on running the same speed as her, she might go for a solid thirteen miles. She'd never competed in a marathon, but she'd run many on her own.

Usually after a difficult case.

"Damn, Wren. How long are you gonna keep this pace up?" Luca sounded winded.

She didn't dare turn her head to look at him. She did not live in the same apartment complex as Luca.

She didn't. She didn't. "I plan to go until I am tired. What are you doing here?"

"Running. I thought that was obvious." He let out a pant but didn't slow his machine down. "You've already done eight miles. How are you not tired?"

Wren shrugged. She was exactly two weeks into her twelve-month lease. Maybe he was closer to his renewal date. With any luck, he'd choose some other place. "When is your lease up?"

She had not meant to ask that.

"I own my apartment. On the top floor." Luca pressed the button to slow his treadmill down as she sped hers up.

Own. *Own. How?*

He was a physical therapist. A darn good one, but he wasn't head of the department. And even if he was, that would still be a hefty mortgage. Though she'd heard about more than one doctor purchasing expensive property and then having basically no furniture while they tried to make payments.

But Luca didn't strike her as the type to make that mistake.

"You shouldn't have told Lena that she could get full range of motion back. She's counting on that."

"Good." Counting on it would make it more likely to happen. Lena needed that mantra because there were going to be days when she wouldn't think it was possible. Days she'd want to give up.

"Damn it, Wren. You can't know that."

"I can." Her feet hit the treadmill one after the other, and she focused on the burn in her limbs to keep her frustration in check. "It is in fact what I was trained to know. And I am very good at my job."

"Her road to recovery—"

"Is going to suck, Luca. I am aware of that. And I made sure she was, too." She blew out a breath. "I am young. I am new to the hospital. But I know a patient capable of full recovery. I will *never* lie to a patient just to make them feel better."

"Wren."

"She can make the recovery, Luca. She believes it, *and* you need to believe it. Period." She sucked in air. It was time to slow down, but her brain refused to lower the speed. "If you can't do it, then I will talk to Therese to ensure she is the only one working with Lena."

"There is no need for that, but absolutes—"

"The world needs some absolutes. Some I am not negotiating." Her heart was pounding in her ears.

The room was silent except for the pounding of their feet against the treads for several minutes.

"I will make sure Lena pushes on the days she wants to give up. And…" the pause hung in the air for a moment "…I owe you an apology. A real one. A heartfelt one. I'm not always a jerk." He huffed out the words as his feet moved forward. "Seriously, I run three miles most days, and my legs are burning."

Wren slowed her machine to a gentle jog and finally turned to look at him. "Why are you so angry at the world?"

Luca blinked several times, and for a moment she feared he was going to slip. "How are you not?"

Wren shrugged. "Ronan would never forgive me if I spent my days wallowing in the unfairness of it all. My parents are living their best life, getting to tell people who I will never meet that they are the sires of a genius. Never mind that they never see me and cut me off when I didn't choose to follow their life plan exactly. Focusing on unhappy memories will not make the world better."

Luca blew out a breath and stopped his treadmill. "I make the world better."

"You do." She slowed the machine down to a brisk walk and took a sip from her water bottle. "But you aren't letting it make you happy."

If he had words for that, he didn't share them. He swiped a towel across his face and stepped off the machine.

By the time she turned off her machine, he was gone.

Wren was making popcorn and dancing to a pop song when a knock on her door echoed through her place.

There was exactly one person who'd be knocking. Apparently, their discussion in the gym an hour ago wasn't enough. She looked at the closed door and weighed leaving it be.

Ronan wouldn't leave it closed.

That was what made her turn the music off and open the door.

Luca stood there, loose blue jeans and soft-looking green T-shirt. It was the half dozen cupcakes in his hands that took her completely off guard.

"Cupcakes?"

He passed them to her. "I said I owed you an apology. Can I come in?"

She stepped back, not sure what to make of the gesture.

"Guess you already have your evening treat. Popcorn. What are you getting ready to watch?"

Wren swallowed. "An animated movie with a singing mermaid."

Her parents had never allowed cartoons for her. Ronan had grown up on the animated movies from the major studios. Wren discovered them two years ago when her roommate pointed out that she wondered if Wren knew what she liked. She'd put the cartoon on to prove a point that Wren couldn't remember now. She'd instantly fallen in love with the music, the cartoons. The documentaries she'd grown up on were fine, but sometimes the brain needed something else.

"Are you purposefully not naming it so I might not recognize that you like a kids movie?"

"There are plenty of adults who like these films. In fact, there are entire online groups." She pursed her lips. This was not something that needed defending. It was a habit she'd gotten into with her parents. They never understood why she'd want to do something "normal," whatever that meant. "I didn't get a lot of kid activities growing up; had to be the genius and all." She let out an uncomfortable laugh. "I never saw the movie, not until I was out of the house. But I wanted the original Princess Ariel mermaid stuffie. Found it online in some resell shop. I have no idea why it called to me, even though I never saw the movie it was based on. But I wanted it so bad. I was getting ready to head to college."

"Which means you were what, ten?" The tone of his voice was harsh.

"Eleven. Almost twelve." She smiled, but he didn't return the look. "Anyway I begged my parents for it as a graduation gift. Silly."

He let out a scoff. "And you didn't get it."

There was no indication he was doing anything other stating a fact. "It wasn't educational." She wasn't sure why she was word vomiting about a mermaid stuffed toy. It wasn't that big of a deal.

The stuffed toy was a symbol. A part of childhood she'd never gotten. A fixture in her mind of the moment she realized her parents cared more for her brain than for her. At least, *academically* she'd understood that. It had taken far longer for her heart to accept that they didn't love her like other parents loved their kids. Even longer to stop trying to earn what wasn't freely given.

Moving to San Diego was the first major step she'd taken since going no contact with them a few years ago. She liked the movie. It was a comfort watch, and she planned to watch it tonight.

Luca took a step closer, a look in his eyes she

couldn't quite decipher. "I haven't seen it in ages, but I remember little girls playing mermaid at the public pool with Ronan and me. Though the play mostly revolved around who could hold their breath their longest."

"And you always won." Back on a neutral topic. That was a blessing.

"How on earth do you remember that? You were still in the toddler pool when Ronan and I were there."

"No. I wasn't there at all. I started reading at two, at an alarming rate, and from that point forward, my free time was dedicated to mental growth. But come on, Luca. You sped up your treadmill to match my speed without any warm-up. And physical therapy school is notoriously difficult to get into. Doesn't take a genius to guess you're competitive."

He chuckled, a deep sound that echoed in the apartment and sent shock waves down her body. The man was stunning. He was also the only person she knew in this city, so having a small crush on the familiarity wasn't surprising.

"I am competitive. But I have also been less than welcoming." He looked at the cupcakes she'd set on her counter. "I'm sorry about that, Wren. Do-over?"

He held his hand out, and she took it without hesitating. "Of course. Want to stay and help me eat all this popcorn?"

She saw him hesitate. The man was on his own. Whether because he liked it that way or for some other reason, she didn't know.

She went to the microwave and grabbed the pop-corn. Holding the bag up, she waved it front of him, "Do I put this in a bowl so we can share, or do my hands get to be the only ones in the bag?"

"Put it in a bowl." He swallowed, like the words had cost him something.

But it was just popcorn and a silly movie with an old friend.

Wren had quietly hummed each of the movie's songs. He was pretty sure if he'd turned down the invitation to stay and watch it with her that she would have belted out the lines from her couch.

She was in his building.

His.

He'd bought the property when an investment company put it up for sale a few years ago. Luca hired a management company to run the daily is-sues and never kept track of who the renters were. But after seeing her in the gym, he'd called the manager to find out Wren's apartment number, so he hadn't had to figure out which was hers.

The credits started rolling, and Wren leaned across him to grab the remote he'd absentmindedly picked up. Her body brushed his for milliseconds, and his heart jumped. This was why he should have told her he had plans when she asked him to stay.

Though she would have known he was lying. The only plans Luca ever had were meetings with his investment advisor every quarter and shifts at the hospital.

And he'd wanted to stay. Wanted to sit closer to her on the couch than he had. Their hands had touched in the popcorn bowl four times. He'd counted.

Ronan's little sister. Not for you.

"Thanks for watching with me." Wren stretched her arms overhead, showing off a thin line of skin as her shirt lifted.

He was thirty-eight years old. He did not need to react to half an inch of skin like a teenage boy.

"Of course." His voice sounded stilted, but if she noticed, Wren didn't say anything. "Next movie night should be at my place."

Why had he said that?

Wren sat up on the couch, grinning from ear to ear. She was so cute. So sweet.

Focus.

"What kind of movies do you like? I'm willing to bet they aren't cartoons?" She pulled her bottom lip through her teeth and let out a sigh.

His mouth was dry. Focusing on anything other than the thump, thump, thump of his heart pounding in his ears was taking all of his strength.

"Or maybe it is? Anime?" She tapped her head, the grin never faltering.

Of course not, she doesn't have any reason to suspect that I'm sitting here getting turned on by just her existence.

"No." He shook his head. "Honestly, I like horror movies. Psychological thrillers. Stuff that makes you jump in a dark room."

Wren giggled. "Ronan used to say he took first dates to horror flicks hoping they'd hop into his arms when they got scared." She pushed his shoulder, then stood. "You aren't trying to get me to jump into your arms, right? Slide from Dr. McSteamy to *Doctor McSteamy*."

The adjustment in tone from playful anger to sultry vixen set his skin ablaze.

"Take a breath, Luca, I'm playing with you." Wren leaned over and grabbed the popcorn bowl before heading to the kitchen.

He took a few deep breaths, not that they steadied him much, then stood. "I knew that."

Wren didn't call him on the lie.

"You talk about Ronan." He barely got his friend's name out. They'd joked about buying houses next to each other. Raising kids together. Brothers from a different mother.

And then he was just gone.

"He's my brother." Wren shrugged. "His life was short. In a couple of years, I will have spent more time without him than I spent with him. Talking about him keeps him alive. Keeps him real."

"I have never had another friend like him." Luca had had no secrets from Ronan. Hell, the man had been with him when the lawyer explained that Aunt Maude had left everything to him. And that *everything* included quite a bit more than the old house the rest of the family grumbled was too big for her, too old, too much.

In other words, they'd wanted her to sell it, so there might be some profit when she was gone.

Ronan understood that Luca would have given it all back if it meant Maude was still there.

The woman made sure he was taken care of. Treated him as more of a son than his parents had. Loved him just for himself. The only family who ever had. And when she'd gotten too fragile to take care of herself, he'd stepped in.

"He was great." Wren stepped into the kitchen. "I'm getting a drink, you want one?"

"What do you have?" He took a few steps, following her. Another moment when he could have stepped away. Another chance to offer an excuse. His colleagues and the half dozen or so women he'd dated for more than two dates complained he was a one-word answer man. Yet around Wren—

"Water, pop, a bottle of wine that I'm saving, so water and pop." She looked at him. "Sorry. I don't do much hosting."

He put an arm around her shoulder, squeezing before his brain had time to think it through. "It's your place. Water is fine. What are you saving the wine for?"

"I don't know." She laughed as she stepped out of his arm. She poured the water and handed him his glass before heading back to the living room with hers.

Color was cresting on her cheeks. Maybe Wren knew the plan for the wine. And whatever it was just didn't include him.

That shouldn't sting. But he wanted to know what she wanted. Wanted to know the joy she was looking forward to. Given how he'd acted, there was no reason for her to share that with him.

"So why San Diego?" She lifted the glass to her lips.

"What?"

Wren shook her head. "Why San Diego? This is literally across the country from where we grew up. And you own your apartment, so obviously you're staying. So why San Diego?"

"Tell you what, you ask me that again in January." He leaned a little closer, then forced himself to pull back. Why was he so drawn to her?

"January? That's nearly six months away." Wren shook her head as she giggled. "Is it that hard of an answer?"

"No." Luca took a sip of water, then set his glass on the coaster. "But you're from Rhode Island, studied and earned your degree from Johns Hopkins in Baltimore and worked in New York City for the last several years. Go through a winter here, then ask me why I stayed."

"You don't miss the snow?" Her eyes widened as she laid her hand on his knee.

Fire. That was the only word to describe the sensation running through his body. The lightning bolt created by her touch. Rather than pull back, he laid his hand on hers and lowered his voice. "You tell me if you miss the snow, the ice, the bone-chilling wind, when you've spent a winter in paradise."

"Paradise." Her mouth slowly formed the word. "That is an awfully big description."

Luca ran his thumb over the soft skin on the back of her hand. "It is. Doesn't make it untrue."

Wren lifted her chin as she pulled away from him. "All right, fine, I will ask you again in January. But then I want a real answer."

There was so much he held back. Truths he spoke to no one. But this one wasn't deep. "I swear, when you get to January, you'll understand."

Wren gave him a playful look. "But that means the two of us will never get to build a snowman. I mean, come on, you have to miss building snowmen."

"When was the last time you built a snowman?"

"Last year!" She put her hands on her hips, a little awkwardly given her position on the couch. "With a few kids from the peds unit. We had a blast. Though the carrot one of the patients borrowed from the cafeteria was a little mushy, pretty sure it was a cooked carrot. Not ideal for a snowman, but it worked in a pinch."

He could see her standing in the hospital courtyard, a heavy coat covering scrubs and snow boots. Laughing with kids. Helping roll the snow for them. A bright snowcap covering her head. The image was cute and fun, and he suddenly wished there was a reason to build a snowman with her.

"I should get going." He was having too much of a good time. Wren was fun, brilliant and gorgeous.

In another time or place, he'd transition this discussion to something far more flirtatious.

Wren's dark hair bounced as she pulled back. "Right, of course."

It felt like an awkward cutoff, but he needed to put distance between them now. His thoughts had slipped past friendly long ago.

Standing, he headed for the door, hearing Wren's soft footsteps behind him. "Thanks for the invitation, Wren." He pulled the door open and stepped out but then turned to lean against the doorjamb. Why was it so difficult to walk away from her?

"Technically you invited yourself. You showed up unannounced *with cupcakes*." She held the door, leaning against it as well.

At least I'm not the only one putting off goodbye. Not that that thought was helpful.

"I said I owed you an apology. And cupcakes are always a good way to say sorry." He playfully rolled his eyes. "*You* invited me to watch the movie."

Wren held up her hands. "Fine. Let's call this one a tie."

He nodded.

"But one more thing." She let out a breath. "Can you recommend a running path? I'm not a huge fan of treadmills, but I don't know the paths around here."

Her free hand was swinging loosely, and his hand itched to reach for it.

"I go for a run before most shifts. I start at five,

do three miles in one of the local parks. I know that isn't a half marathon, but—"

"You going tomorrow morning?"

"Meet you here?" He should have said he'd meet her in the lobby. Set some form of boundary. But no. The words were out, and there was no reason to withdraw them. Even if he wanted to…which he very much did not.

"I will be ready at five till five." She pursed her lips. "This is turning into a Midwestern goodbye."

He raised a brow.

"One of my roommates in New York, Rebecca, she was from Ohio. I used to joke that it took her thirty minutes to tell everyone she was leaving and another twenty to actually walk out the door." She gestured between the two of them. "Like we're doing. She swore it was a thing, even an expectation where she was from."

Luca grinned. "Good night, Wren." The words were hard to say, but it was time to step away.

"Good night, Luca."

CHAPTER FIVE

WREN STRETCHED AND waited for the knock on the door as she replayed the evening. They'd started off uncomfortable. Her calling him out in the gym. That had somehow turned into him bringing her cupcakes and watching a kids movie with her.

Parts of the night had felt like flirting. Right? She didn't have much experience with that, so maybe she was reading into the long goodbye. The subtle leans toward her.

Ugh. Overthinking it wasn't going to help anything. And neither was waiting by the door. She stepped out of her apartment, locked the door, then hooked her keys on her hydration belt.

Luca was already walking down the hallway. The man was punctual, she'd give him that.

"A hydration belt with multiple water bottles? I thought we were going for a short jog?"

Wren stepped beside him as they started down the stairs to the first floor. "I need it for long runs, and it seemed silly to buy more than one running belt, so I use it for all runs." That wasn't the whole truth, but it wasn't a lie, either. "Good news is, it makes me feel weird if I leave one empty. Your lucky day. If you get thirsty, I have an extra filled and ready to go."

"Makes you feel weird to leave one empty or at home?"

They stepped into the crisp morning air, and Wren grinned. He wasn't wrong about the nice weather.

"Yeah. I always fill both. Habit, but once I form one, I have a hard time breaking it." Wren pulled her hands over her head, then gestured to the street. "Which way we off to?"

Luca tilted his head, then set off at a steady pace. "Park trail is this way. Why do you have a hard time breaking a habit?"

She fell into pace beside him. "What?" She'd heard the question but needed a moment to think of an answer. Because this wasn't really about habits.

"Why do you have a hard time breaking habits? I mean, other than the fact that habits, by their nature, are difficult to break. Thus the reason they are called habits." He turned his head and grinned, but there was a look in his eye that made her glance away.

"As you said, habits by their nature are difficult to break." If only she'd just stated that fact.

"Come on, Wren," Luca pressed as their feet hit the pavement.

"Ronan always had to do things certain ways. Remember?" She wasn't sure Luca would recall the issue. Her brother probably had a form of obsessive-compulsive disorder. Not that their parents ever had him checked. He was *normal*—their word—and therefore boring.

Her brother was anything but boring. And if he'd gotten his chance, she was sure he'd have gotten at least a few seasons in the majors. Whether he could have made the hall of fame or not, who knew? But until he did something extraordinary, their parents largely ignored him.

"Yeah." Luca huffed out a breath as his feet fell into the same rhythm as hers. "He had some things that, if they got messed up, sent him into a spiral. He was working with a therapist on it."

"He was?" Ronan had never shared that with her. Though, when he'd passed, she was sixteen. That wasn't necessarily something one shared with such a little sister.

"Yeah. His team found a therapist, and they were having success overcoming what was habit and what was compulsive." He looked at her again, and this time the look was very brotherly. "Do you struggle with compulsive thoughts?"

"No." She didn't like that look. Didn't appreciate the tone change, either. "But this is Ronan's belt. He's the one I started running with. And he always, always had to have both bottles full. So." She shrugged.

They ran in silence for a few minutes before he turned onto a smaller path. "Come on, I want to show you something."

They ran until they were on a clearing overlooking the San Diego Bay. The sun was starting to rise, causing glittery beams across the water.

"The sunset is prettier. After all, it sets right

over the bay, but I like the shine it gives as it starts to rise."

"It is gorgeous." Wren wrapped her arms around herself, very aware of the man standing next to her. Aware that she wanted more of the flirtatious tone from last night. And none of the protective tone he'd slipped into. "Thanks for bringing me. We'll have to come back at sunset."

"Sure." Luca looked at her and took a deep breath and leaned toward her.

He's about to kiss me.

She hadn't misread the signs last night.

"Luca." She leaned toward him, putting her hand on his chest. How did he kiss? Soft and slow? Passionate and demanding?

"I know Ronan isn't around, and your parents are your parents, so if you need someone…"

She dropped her hand and pulled back. How had she misread this so badly? Her mouth was dry, and if the earth opened beneath her right now, she'd gladly step into the hole to get away.

"I mean, I owe Ronan to look after you."

Owe Ronan. Not for her. Not really.

"Stop." She backed away as the word fell from her lips.

Misreading the signs about what he wanted was bad enough, but San Diego was supposed to be a fresh start. A place where she wasn't seen as the naive genius. Despite all her accomplishments, people still saw the scared nineteen-year-old resident standing next to the men and women who'd started med school at the traditional age.

It was nice that Luca was here. More than nice, but if he saw her as a duty…a person needing protection… Her stomach rolled. She'd thought maybe—

No. She wasn't traveling down that road.

She loved her brother and hated how his name had disappeared from everyone's lips weeks after his funeral. A ghost no one wanted to bring up.

She'd thought the two of them were reminiscing. It was refreshing that Luca spoke of him. But she wanted to be Wren to Luca. Her own person with a shared history and exciting future.

Such a lovely thought but apparently not reality. To him, she was Ronan's little sister. A debt he owed a friend. A burden. Though she knew he'd never use those words. But it wasn't possible to pay off a debt to a ghost.

"Wren."

She shook her head, pushing off whatever he planned to say. "I wanted a friend, not a brotherly protector. So uh, yeah. I'm going to head back now. Thanks for showing me where to come to watch the sunrise and sunset on my runs. I'll see you around the hospital."

Then she turned on her heel and headed back down the trail.

Luca had gone all day without seeing Wren. And he'd looked for her.

His offer this morning had been stupid. He'd

never replace her brother. And he damn well didn't want the position. He'd done it to remind himself who she was.

Because the sunbeams hitting her cheeks this morning had sent a wave of longing through him. He dreamed of kissing her, every night. Dreamed of sliding his lips down that soft neck. Then she'd put her hand on his chest. He'd had to remind himself somehow.

He cleared his throat as he climbed the stairs. He was checking in on Lena. She'd proudly showed him she was ready for a new ball this morning. A shock considering she'd had that one for less than twenty-four hours. But she was determined.

Wren had done that.

He knocked, then entered Lena's room, tossing the ball up in the air. "Here it is. I want to make sure you know that it may take you several days or even a week to level up from this ball. This is a marathon, not a sprint."

Lena took the ball, a frown crossing her lips.

"You all right?" The woman was never perky with him. Most of his patients rolled their eyes when he pushed them to do one more exercise. Physical therapy was tough, physically and mentally. He never took it personally. But there was something about her expression.

"Dr. Freson was just in here."

He waited a minute, but when she didn't elaborate, he pushed, "Did Dr. Freson have concerns about your wound?" He'd checked the notes before coming up here—if Wren was worried she'd not said anything in the notes. Though if she just left, she wouldn't have had a chance to update them.

Lena rolled the ball around her palm. "She was kind and said my hand looked good, no sign of infection."

All of that was good news. "That is what you should expect to hear. Burns are notorious for infections. It's what Dr. Freson will focus on most."

He understood that not every day netted fresh news. That was rough, but it was to be expected.

"It's not that." Lena squeezed the ball and didn't hide the wince. "She wasn't her sunshiny self."

Their talk this morning was certainly rough. He hadn't meant to upset her. A routine he was breaking with her *now*. "I'll check on her." He'd planned to give her space today. Give himself space to acknowledge the desire she raised in him. But if she was upset, he wasn't waiting.

"Thanks. Her happiness is infectious. I don't think she realizes that. Plus, she's my favorite doctor. I don't want her sad."

Luca laid a hand across his heart and gave a playful wounded sound. "*She* is your favorite? What about me?"

"You're nice, but it's no competition." Lena squeezed the ball again and huffed as she released it. "You're kind of a torture artist."

"Kinda. But it gets results." He winked, then headed out of the room.

"Luca." Therese was marching up the hallway.

"You should head back to the physio room using that stairwell." She pointed to the door she'd probably exited from.

"Why?"

"Call it a feeling." She nodded and walked away, never looking back.

He looked at the stairs and headed for them. Pushing the door open, he headed down the first flight and saw Wren looking out the window. That particular window showcased the parking lot, so it certainly wasn't for the view.

"You all right?"

"No." Wren shook her head but didn't elaborate.

"Is it about this morning?" A dumb question. One he regretted as soon as her eyes turned toward him.

The tears hadn't fallen, but they were clear in her dark eyes.

"Luca, this morning was uncomfortable and awkward, nothing more." Even with tears in her eyes, it was said with a kindness he didn't deserve.

"Fair." He moved to stare out the same window. "Not the hospital's best view."

"No. But it works in a pinch." She let out a sigh. "Difficult patient. A surgery didn't go as planned. It happens." She blinked a few times, then took a deep breath. So much unsaid but communicated in those words. "Have a good day, Doctor." She started for the stairs, but he couldn't let her go. Not yet.

He grabbed her hand, as stunned by the action as her wide eyes indicated she was. "I like spending time with you."

She nodded but didn't add anything to the conversation.

"Not because of Ronan. I like just hanging out with you. It's easy." He was rambling. "What I mean is that I said a dumb thing. I want to be friends."

It would be easy to want more with Wren. But he wasn't going to focus on that.

She looked at his hand holding hers. "Actual friends?" She hesitated a minute before adding, "Not stepping into a position I don't need filled?" Wren arched her brow, but she didn't pull away.

"Yeah. In fact, why don't we do movie night again? My place this time. I think I promised you a horror movie. Though if your day's been bad—"

"Sounds great. What time?" Wren finally pulled her hand from his.

He looked at their separated hands, instantly missing the connection. "Seven? I'll order dinner delivery." That made it sound almost like a date.

Because part of me wishes it was.

"Okay. I'm not a picky eater, so whatever you want is fine. I'll cash you some funds."

She was obviously not thinking it was anything but two awkward friends hanging out. "You are my guest, Wren."

"All right."

"Before you go…" He was seeing her in a few hours. There was no reason to slow her down. "I gave Lena a new workout ball. She's made excellent progress in just a day. You were right. She is going to get full range of motion back. Fast, too, if she puts as much effort into it as she did yesterday."

Wren bit her lip rather than smiling. That meant she was probably thinking the same thing he was. It was fast, but plateaus happened. "She's going to hit at least one wall. And when she does, maybe Therese can play good physical therapist and you play bad guy. Let Therese be her outlet to complain to, while you keep pushing her to get where she wants."

It was a good idea. A great one. "I don't think Therese knows any other role but good guy. And I am the resident grump, so it makes sense."

Wren tilted her head, a tiny frown appearing. "You aren't a grump. Or rather you are."

He playfully hit his chest again, this time pretending that Wren was the one wounding him. "The sunshiny surgeon thinks I'm a grump."

"You just called yourself a grump." She wagged a finger at him. "But you aren't really. You just don't like to show this side of you to everyone else. Maybe you should."

He almost wanted to give a little salute at the request. Instead, Luca shrugged. "I am who I am."

"I think you have layers." Wren looked at her watch and headed for the door. "I want popcorn if you're going to make me watch a horror flick. Only fair."

Only fair indeed.

CHAPTER SIX

You sure you don't want to cancel? I know the surgery took more than five hours. You must be exhausted.

Luca looked the text over and then forced himself to hit Send. He should have sent it before he left the hospital. The last thing Wren probably wanted was a movie night after today.

That afternoon, a car caught fire on Interstate 15, and Wren and two other surgeons had treated the trapped patient. He'd heard through the hospital grapevine that it was touch-and-go, but touch-and-go meant still alive. After the rough surgery at the start of her shift, a movie night was probably the last thing she wanted.

Headed up now. Unless you and Hippo need a night off.

Nope.

He looked over at the dog snoring—loudly—on the giant bed Luca purchased for him last year. He'd bounce up when Wren got here and then sleep through their movie.

Movie. Wren.

All right, he grabbed the popcorn kernels and threw them in the fancy maker he'd bought himself last Christmas so he could start them as soon as they were ready for the flick. There was exactly no reason for him to have a movie theater-grade machine in the theater room. Particularly since, after Wren's arrival, he'd have hosted exactly one person in it.

But as a kid he'd always joked that one day he'd make movie theater buttered popcorn any time he wanted. A joke that made Maude laugh until she started coughing. She'd told him that she believed he'd have it one day. The only hint he'd had about the wealth she was hiding.

He'd put off the purchase. But then, on the anniversary of her death a few years ago, he'd given into the whim, promptly made six batches of popcorn, then let it largely collect dust. A problem he'd fixed as soon as he got home today.

It was shiny and ready now.

The doorbell rang, and Luca headed to pick up his guest, Hippo catching up to him before he opened the door.

Her stomach said hello before Wren could get a word out. "Don't suppose you ordered food already? Guess I was hungrier than expected."

Hippo pressed against her legs. Wren dropped down and gave him attention. Then her stomach let out another gurgle.

"Bed, Hippo."

The dog gave him pouty eyes, but he followed

the command and headed back to his bed, looking over his shoulder at Wren the whole time.

Luca stepped back to let her in. "I've got sushi and fried rice. You said you weren't picky."

"Poor Hippo."

"Poor Hippo, nothing. He's already had his dinner and a treat. You're the one who needs to eat. So, is what I ordered okay?"

"Sounds perfect." Her stomach grumbled again.

"Pretty sure you'd say it was perfect no matter what I had, given what your stomach is saying." Luca chuckled and led her to the kitchen.

He turned, surprised to find her still standing several feet behind him.

"You own the whole floor." Her eyes roamed the entry and living room with its huge windows overlooking the San Diego Bay.

"Come on, you're starving. We can talk real estate while you eat." He reached for her hand and pulled her along.

"Yeah, but this is the whole floor!" Wren's voice was soft, and she was staring out the window as he led the way. "I mean I only saw one door, but somehow it didn't register until just now."

The view was why he'd purchased the building. It was one of his favorite places. There was a little pit in his stomach as he watched her. Was Wren piecing together what it meant that he owned the floor?

She stopped in front of the window for just a minute. "Man, I was excited I paid my med school loans down enough to afford to rent my place. This is so impressive."

Med school loans.

Something most physicians carried well into their late thirties. Though he would have expected a genius to get most of her bills paid for by scholarships. Or her parents, they could certainly have afforded it.

A chill went down his spine. Would she become someone different, someone who only looked at him for his wallet, like everyone else when she figured it out?

I don't want to lose her.

He wasn't sure how to process that thought, so he let go of her hand and pointed toward the dining room. "Come on, let's get you fed. I got a whole selection of sushi. And the fried rice." He set the bowl out, then placed the sushi board to her across the table.

Wren looked from the sushi to the fried rice, then to him. "Selection is certainly the word." She grabbed a pair of chopsticks and dug in.

For several minutes, they sat in silence, munching on food.

But far too soon, she leaned back and gestured to the apartment. "How? I mean, physical therapy pays, but I mean—" Wren opened her arms wider. "How?"

"An investment hit big." Heat was in his cheeks. Not a complete lie. He'd made some very good decisions with Maude's inheritance. But it wasn't exactly the truth. Was this the moment? The transition? The change?

"I'd say so." She looked toward the window.

He held his breath. He'd gone through this countless times. If it happened again, he'd figure it out.

Somehow.

"Not sure I'd ever leave the view." Wren put her head on her hands, gazing out at the bay. Then she looked back at him, her dark gorgeous gaze holding him tight. "How much do you want me to send you? What cash app do you use?"

For a second, he wasn't sure he'd heard the question right. He might not have hosted anyone in the theater room, but many dates and a few men he thought might be friends had made it to this table. And each one saw the view and pieced together what it meant. No one who crossed his threshold ever offered to pay for anything.

A couple of fingers snapped in front of him. "Earth to Luca."

"Sorry, you're good. I told you. You're my guest."

"I know you said that, but you must have bought the entire sushi menu." She waved at the still very full plate of food. "I can pony up some coin to cover it."

Her grin struck his heart. "Nope. I got this. You had two long surgeries." He never minded paying; it was the audacity to assume that it was his only role in any relationship that had him cut everyone out.

"Fine. But…" she stood, grabbing her plate "…my treat next time."

Her hip brushed his as she stepped around him, a lightning bolt of desire streaking across his skin.

"So, where in this cavernous place are we watching a horror movie?"

"I have a theater room."

Wren giggled as she rinsed her plate and put it in the dishwasher. "*Of course* you have a theater room! As long as there's popcorn."

"I promised." He started to reach for her hand to lead her toward the theater room but caught himself. Barely. He'd already held it once. He did not need to do so. Not again.

Wren looked at his hand but didn't reach for him.

"This way." They entered the theater, and he immediately walked over to the popcorn machine and flipped it on.

"Get out! I always wanted one of these. Always. I mean, how are you not eating popcorn ALL THE TIME?" She clapped her hands and bounced as the corns started popping out of the oil.

"Who says I'm not eating it all the time?" There was no way to stop the grin on his face. Wren's brightness was infectious.

"Fair."

He pushed a few buttons, and the screen rolled down.

"You might get sick of me. Because anytime I want to see a movie, I am knocking on your door. No more microwave popcorn for me." She reached for the salt shaker by the machine, then hesitated, "Can I?"

"Why not?"

"Perfect answer." She salted the popcorn, filled the bowl he'd left by the machine, then turned to him, popping a piece through her perfect lips immediately. "Showtime."

He only had a small couch in the center of the room. He'd planned to put in theater chairs, but the realization that others wouldn't sit in them had stopped the acquisition. A sad little fact he wasn't upset about now.

Wren sat on the couch, and he slid in next to her.

"You are in charge of popcorn." She pressed the bowl into his hands. The brush of her fingers against his drove his pulse up.

"Don't trust yourself with it?" He looked at the bowl, then back at her. Not that he'd minded, but she'd gripped her bowl so tightly the other night he assumed she'd want full control of it.

Last night. He was at her place last night.

Time moved swiftly and also, somehow, slowed when Wren was with him.

"I get jumpy in these types of movies. There's a good chance we'll end up with more popcorn on the floor than in our bellies." She chuckled and looked away, color staining her cheeks.

Luca put his hand on her chin, turning her to look at him. "We can pick any other movie. This—"

"Does the killer get what's coming to him in this?" She didn't pull away from his touch.

Luca's thumb traced the edge of her jaw. What would happen if he replaced it with his mouth?

Focus. "Spoiler, but yes. It's a very campy movie, but there's blood, gore and jump scares."

"Perfect. I want an outlet for my feelings. A justified ending. I can handle it." She put her hand on his knee. "But I am staying right next to you during this flick. And not just because you have the smallest couch ever in here."

Luca put his arm around her shoulder. "That is perfectly fine."

"Eeek!" Wren pinched her eyes closed as she leaned her head against Luca's shoulder—again. She'd spent more time in this position than any other.

Maybe this movie hadn't been such a good choice. She'd wanted something different. Something to take her mind off the day. A different reason for her dreams to have a haunting quality to them than the day she'd had.

Her first surgery was for a skin graft failure. The infection spread was more than she'd anticipated, so amputation was the only option. Her role in the second was more as an aid to the general surgeon. The patient wasn't stable enough to worry about plastics, but the surgeon had wanted her expertise for the burns that covered more than forty percent of his body.

A young man. Newly engaged. Life forever changed. His fiancée had not taken the news well. In fact, Wren watched her slip the ring off her finger as she walked out of the room where they'd gone over the surgery details with her.

The patient wasn't even awake, and the woman he planned to spend the rest of his life wasn't going to meet him at the altar. The life he'd planned was over.

She'd learned long ago that life wasn't fair. She didn't let the fact steal her joy. That didn't mean tough cases didn't puncture the happy bubble she kept around her.

Luca squeezed her shoulder. "The killer is about to get their due, if you want to watch?"

She turned her head but didn't lift it. She peeked through her eyes and watched the final battle come to a satisfying end. "Sorry I spent most of the time burying my head. I admit that was scarier than I anticipated."

"We watched an animated film yesterday. I should have started with something lighter." He chuckled but didn't pull away from her.

She let out a breath. "I pushed it. I mean, you offered, and I was all like…" Wren lifted her head and pointed to herself as she mimicked the tone she'd used earlier, "…*I can handle it*. The one thing I will never understand is why every horror flick starts with an easy out. I mean all the hero had to do was *not* say the cursed words. He knew he was cursed, but *no*—"

"Humans are selfish at their core. He knew he was cursed, but he didn't really believe it. He thought he'd be different. He'd be the one to make the change. That the rules didn't apply to him."

The words were sharp. Pointed. A full-on critique

she'd not expected. "I don't think that's fair. I mean, curses aren't real—"

"Oh, I disagree there."

She laid her hand over his chest. "You are not cursed." Wren wasn't sure why she said the words. They sounded silly, but he didn't laugh or give her any indication that he agreed with her statement.

He started to shrug, then must have realized her head was still on his shoulder.

She needed to move. *Why is it so hard to pull away?* Waiting wasn't going to make it easier, so Wren forced herself to pull back.

Did he frown?

His shoulder is probably sore from hosting my head.

Don't read into things, Wren.

He wanted friendship. He'd made that clear. Just because her heart danced around him didn't mean he felt the same. "Sorry. Movie over, no reason to crowd your space."

"You can bury your head in my shoulder any-time, Wren." Luca leaned toward her.

Her skin burned as her gaze focused on his full lips.

He pushed a loose hair behind her ear. A *very* friendly gesture.

"I should get going." The words tasted like ash, but she forced them out. There was no reason to think Luca had any interest in kissing her. She'd practically forced her way into his life.

There is no "practically" to it.

The man was hot. He was smart. He was kind—when he let people in. The perfect crush candidate.

He stood, and she followed suit. She had said she needed to go. No sense dragging it out.

Still, she wandered over to Hippo. The dog had slept through the whole movie and only opened one eye as she rubbed his head. But his tail happily whapped against the bed.

"Does he have a fancy bed in every room?" She rubbed his head once more, then stood. She'd seen a bed in the living room, the dining room and a small one in the corner of the kitchen that she couldn't imagine the goober ever curling up in.

"Yes. Oh no. The guest bathroom is bed-free. But no one ever uses it, so not sure that counts." Luca winked and put his hands in his pockets. He didn't head for the door, and she didn't move, either.

"Thank you for hosting me. I meant it… My treat next time. You can even bring Hippo for dinner. Though you will have to bring a bed. I don't have one."

"You ever wanted a dog?" His gaze darted to Hippo, then back to her.

"You offering this sweet boy?" she playfully teased as she stepped closer to Luca and put her hands in her pockets, mimicking him. It also meant she couldn't easily touch him.

Luca opened his mouth, making a horrified face she knew was all for show. "Of course not. He's my baby."

Loves dogs.

Another mental box checked on the crush list.

"My parents never let us have an animal. They promised Ronan once that if he got a perfect score card, he could get a cat."

"I remember that." Luca let out a sigh. "He had it, too. Except he forgot a math assignment on the last day of the quarter."

"He didn't forget it." The old anger surged in her chest. Her parents had casually let the secret out of the bag after he passed. "Mom took it out of his backpack while he was making his lunch."

"What!" Luca swallowed as the word echoed around him.

"Yeah. They didn't want a cat. So Mom sabotaged him." She pulled her hands from her pockets and wrapped her arms around herself. "She told me about it a few years ago. Last time I talked to them. All they ever cared about was achievement, but when he was on the cusp of a truly impressive feat, they swiped it away from him."

She took a deep breath, shocked at the words spilling from her. But the dam was broken, and more flowed forth. "It was one thing to say stuffed animals for a genius were unnecessary or to never celebrate birthdays or—"

"Never celebrate birthdays?"

"Yeah, well. They only ever saw my mind." Wren shrugged. "I spent all night with my head buried in your shoulder. Now I'm spilling my guts in your theater room." She looked around the room. "This really is impressive, Luca."

He shifted his feet, color rising in his cheeks. "Thanks."

"I should get going."

"You already said that." He took a step toward her but didn't lead the way to the front door.

"I did." There was so little distance between them. The room was suddenly hot. She watched his eyes lower, looking at her lips. Wren wanted far too badly to believe he was thinking of kissing her.

She'd kissed a few men. Brief kisses ending a second date. Awkward moments that always ended her desire to have a third.

Wren's body ached with need as he shifted. If he lowered his head, their lips would touch.

Or if I lift myself up.

"Luca—"

"Wren?"

He had not been called, but Hippo let out his own bray at the moment, and both of them jumped back. The dog wagged his tail, and he pushed himself between them.

That was probably for the best. She'd never had a second kiss. And she wanted Luca in her life now that she'd found him again.

But part of her wished Hippo had waited a second before making his presence known. At least then she'd know if Luca had wanted to kiss her. Or if it was just in her mind.

"That is my cue." She smiled down at Hippo, then nodded to Luca. "Thanks again for tonight."

"Any time." This time he stepped around her and

led her out of the room and right to the front door. No hesitation. No stretching things out this time. "Sweet dreams, Wren."

She stepped out, and the door closed behind her.

Wren stood there for a moment, a finger to her lips. Then she shook her head. With any luck, her dreams would be filled with Luca instead of the horror movie or today's highlights from the hospital.

CHAPTER SEVEN

LUCA LOOKED TOWARD the door of the therapy room, very aware that Wren had not stopped in.

"When is Wren coming by?"

It was like Therese had read his mind. Which meant he was obvious enough about who he was hoping might pay a visit.

"No idea." He looked back at the file on the tablet. He had three more patients this afternoon. "Why are you asking?"

"Because you keep looking at that door. Plus, she usually stops by around now. Wren is fun. And I enjoy her company." Therese went to grab a bench for her next patient.

"Wren is fun." Luca moved without thinking. Therese was pregnant, and she did not need to move all the heavy equipment on her own.

"I could have done that on my own." Therese shook her head as he grabbed the other end of the bench. "But thank you."

Luca nodded.

"Any chance I can get the chatty version that appears with Wren?" Therese chuckled, but it sounded forced.

"What?"

They set the bench down, and she crossed her arms. "Come on. You really don't see it, McSteamy?"

He looked to the door...again. No Wren. Damn. He didn't realize how much he missed the bright ray of sunshine she brought when she entered the room. "No."

"That." Therese pointed at him. "That right there."

"What?"

Therese pinched the bridge of her nose. "Seriously. She is the only one who can get more than a few words out of you. I take it as a personal win if I manage more than three words at a time."

Luca crossed his arms, not enjoying the statement. He chatted. Sort of. "I speak with my patients all the time."

"Yes. It's the reason so many people like you. But none of us can get close to you. The best we can do is know that you live on coffee. Which almost everyone in this place does, so that isn't exactly personal insight. No one knows where you live, if you're married or seeing someone."

"I'm not." He hadn't meant to comment. His love life was a dismal record.

One broken engagement—on his wedding day. A handful of uneventful dates. One of whom became interested in him only after she'd done some digging on him. Luca still wasn't sure how the woman found out his exact net worth, but it was clear that she'd changed her tune when the dollar signs appeared. He'd had to hire security for the apartment building because she kept finding ways into it.

No one had gotten close in years. That was easier than losing people when they discovered the truth.

"So you aren't dating Wren?" Therese raised her brow.

Dating Wren?

His body heated as his tongue tried to force out the word *no*. They were friends. Only friends.

Though over the last two weeks, they'd spent nearly every minute outside the hospital together. She'd "repaid" the sushi by cooking him pasta. He'd asked her to come on evening walks with Hippo. Last night, she'd even showed off the dog bed she purchased for Hippo, so Luca didn't have to keep bringing one down. Hippo had certainly approved.

"No." The word burned. "We are simply friends." *Simply.*

He cared about her. She was hot. And funny, sweet. *And my dead best friend's sister.* That was against the code. You didn't date little sisters. At least not without asking. And there was no way to find out if Ronan was okay with the idea.

Therese let out a laugh. "Yeah. I used to say the same about Seth." She rubbed her belly to emphasize how much that relationship had shifted. "Now we're expecting and trying to figure out where we're going to put the crib in Seth's cramped apartment."

"Well, Wren and I are just friends." The words nearly stuck in his throat, but he got them out.

His dreams were haunted by her. There was nothing friendly about those, and he relished the night knowing for a few hours his mind could hold what his soul wouldn't.

"Great." Therese smirked. "So you don't mind if Seth and I set her up with a friend of his?"

His soul screamed no. But that wasn't fair to Wren. She was wonderful. She deserved a partner who worshipped her.

I could do that.

"Which friend?" Like he'd know whoever the answer was. Luca knew his colleagues…as colleagues.

"Dr. Griffen."

He knew that one. "The playboy in peds. Absolutely not." Luca was shocked that Therese would even suggest such a thing.

Matt Griffen was nice and a great pediatrician. He was also known for having dated the most nurses, doctors and other staff in the hospital. Luca had even heard that HR had a discussion with him following the rumor he'd dated the entire phlebotomy staff. He'd politely told them that he had in fact only dated three fourths of the staff. And to the best of his knowledge, there were no complaints.

That was the thing. No one ever said anything untoward went down. Just that the man was *never* settling. Wren did not deserve to be another notch in his bedpost.

"Dr. Reeves is single."

"He's been divorced less than a month." Luca was incensed on Wren's behalf. She was not rebound material.

"I wasn't aware you followed hospital gossip so closely."

He raised a brow. "I hear things."

"Mm-hmm. What about Scott Rogers?"

Luca opened his mouth, then shut it. The emergency room nurse was great. He'd heard nothing but nice things about him. *Damn it.*

"Anyone want a coffee?" Wren walked in, coffee carrier in hand. "Oh. Sorry. I clearly caught you two deep in conversation."

"You didn't." Luca rushed the words out as his shoulders relaxed seeing her smile.

"I was talking to Luca about setting you up with one of Seth's friends." Therese smiled at him, a dare clear in her eyes.

Wren's eyes shifted to Therese, then to him. There was something unsaid in those eyes. Something that made his stomach drop.

"You were talking about setting me up?" The question was aimed at him.

"Therese was discussing it."

"And Luca was shooting down everyone I suggested." The physical therapist stepped toward Wren.

"Shooting them down?" Wren looked at him, swallowing.

"None of them are good enough for you. As I was explaining to Therese." This was a minefield.

Wren opened her mouth, then closed it.

He was pretty sure that he'd just stepped on a pin.

"I'm sorry, Wren. Seth and I were talking, and we

thought maybe…but…" Therese sucked in a deep breath, her cheeks darkening. "I see three cups. Any chance one of those is decaf?"

Wren nodded as she handed Therese her coffee, but she still didn't say anything.

Therese hesitated for a second. "I'm sorry. I overstepped. I appreciate the coffee, and I hope our new friendship is okay."

Wren's dark gaze held his. "I don't date." She swallowed and turned her sunshine toward Therese.

"Oh." Therese shook her head. "Got it."

Don't date? What the hell did she mean by that?

"But you didn't know that. And of course we're fine." Wren reached her hand out and squeezed Therese's arms, "I heard Becky in radiology complaining that all her matches on a dating app were coming up duds. I bet she would love a setup. But not with Dr. Griffen. Apparently, she is well aware of his reputation." Wren smiled at Therese. A genuine smile that Luca suspected she didn't plan to direct toward him.

"His reputation does precede him." Therese looked at her watch and cleared her throat. "Speaking of peds, I need to see a patient up there now. You might want to call the floor, Luca. I would have thought your patient would be down by now." Therese used the excuse to make a quick escape.

Luca walked over to the terminal to give the third floor nurses station a ring. Therese was right. His patient should be here by now. If Mrs. Johnson had a holdup, he needed to know.

"Here's your coffee." Wren set it on the terminal, then turned to go.

He reached for her free hand, gripping it tight. "Wait a minute, please." He held his breath as Wren looked at the door, clearly weighing heading out.

When she turned to face him, Luca sighed into the phone.

"Quite the sigh, Dr. McDonnell," the voice on the other end said. "We are still bringing Mrs. Johnson, but the porter is running behind." The nurse didn't offer a goodbye after imparting the information. Fair. They were more than busy.

He put the phone down, then turned all his focus to Wren. But before he could get any words out, she started in on him.

"You want to explain why you shot everyone down?" Her chin was raised, daggers shooting directly at him. Not the sunshiny reaction he enjoyed getting from her.

"What does it matter? You don't date. Why?"

"I told you I wanted a friend. Not a protector. I don't need protecting. I don't need you vetting my dating life." She bit her lip and looked at the door but still didn't start for it. "I am in charge of my life."

"I wasn't protecting you. I mean. I was. Dr. Griffen has dated most of the eligible members of the hospital. Which you clearly know, and Dr. Reeves is looking for a rebound after his wife left him." He had no answer for Scott in ER, so he left him out. Luca took advantage of Wren not adding to the conversation to press her again. "Why don't you date?"

"Because." She shrugged but didn't add anything else. "I stopped by Lena's room. They're prepping her for discharge, but she'll still come here for therapy, right?"

Luca didn't enjoy the shift of topic, but he let it go for the minute. They were supposed to have dinner tonight. Her place again. She'd promised him pho and chocolate cake.

Tonight he'd figure out the answer behind that because…

Why?

He didn't want to press too much at that mental question.

"Yes. I think it would be helpful if we can schedule her at a time when you can see the progress. She's concerned the scar tissue is limiting her movement."

Wren's brows furrowed. "Scar tissue moves differently. You know that."

"I know. And I have told her that more than once, but hearing it from the expert…" He gestured to her and gave a little bow. Usually, it made her smile, but today her lips didn't crack at all.

"Wren—"

"Dr. McDonnell." Mrs. Johnson clapped to get his attention. She'd finally arrived. "Watch." It took the elderly Black woman a moment, but she pushed herself into a standing position with no help from the porter.

Wren clapped. "Way to go. I can see how hard you worked on that." Then without telling Luca goodbye, she headed out.

"What a nice woman," Mrs. Johnson remarked.

"That is Dr. Freson. One of the plastic surgeons here." Luca stepped up to his patient.

"Well, nice, beautiful and smart. Sounds like the whole package."

She is.

Luca looked at the distance between himself and Mrs. Johnson. "I am here to catch you, but can you take two steps for me?"

"I can tell a subject change when I hear one, young man." Mrs. Johnson let out a chuckle as she resolutely took one slow step forward.

Wren rolled her head on her shoulders, trying to relieve the knot so that maybe she could focus on the scans in front of her. Charlie Simpson's body was rejecting the skin graft her plastic surgeon had done three years ago following a skin cancer diagnosis.

The plastic surgeon had used Charlie's skin. So it should have healed quicker. The body rejecting its own skin was rare, though it happened.

This felt off. The rejection should have happened sooner, and part of the skin looked like it wasn't rejected. It was a puzzle, and she couldn't figure out what she was missing.

The door opened, but she didn't turn.

"Sorry, I didn't realize anyone was in here." Seth Graham started to close the door, then stepped back in. He stood quietly looking at the scans. "Rejection issue?"

"Yes." It was good he was here. Maybe another pair of eyes could see what she kept missing. Wren pointed to the left side of the graft. "But here the tissue looks fine. I've never seen it reject like this."

Seth tilted his head, his eyes roaming the image. "Each rejection is different."

That was true, but she could usually spot the pattern. Figure it out instantly. A gift and a curse. Today the image was stumping Wren. Her head was almost stuffy. Like the neurons wouldn't quite fire.

Because I burned too many out focusing on Luca's conversation with Therese.

"The blood flow is off here."

As soon as Seth said it, her eyes snapped to the location. That was it. That was what was keeping her rooted in this spot. "Not by much." She looked at the tiny vessels in Charlie's cheeks. They were delivering blood flow but not enough. "Impressive catch."

"You'd have figured it out." Seth stepped up and pointed at the area on the left of the graft. "I bet one of the vessels hooked up here failed."

Wren knew she'd have eventually caught it, but the pros of having another pair of eyes take a look could not be overstated.

"There are so many tiny vessels there. Usually the body would compensate, but in this instance it didn't happen."

Which meant it was possible it might happen

again. "What would you do to ensure blood flow next time?"

"You're the plastics genius."

She mentally bristled at the word. *Genius*. The tag assigned to her before she understood its full meaning. The tag that still kept her as an other.

Wren refused to refer to herself as a genius. Her mind was a steel trap, but there were so many things she didn't know. Other experts she deferred to. That tag interfered with everything from friends to her nonexistent dating life.

"Humor me, Dr. Graham. You are hardly a junior plastics resident."

Seth sighed, a sound she knew was a precursor to an uncomfortable truth. "I don't know, honestly. The graft looks like it was well done. Sometimes these things just don't work."

Such an unsatisfying truth. People expected doctors to have all the answers. She had a lot of answers but not all of them.

"You all right?" Seth was still looking at the images on the screen, but she felt him shift beside her.

"Fine. I just…" She hesitated and then figured his fiancée was likely to fill him in on everything anyway. "Therese told me about your plan to set me up with Dr. Griffen."

"What?" Seth's voice echoed in the small room before he cleared his throat. "Sorry, I mean, what are you talking about? I would never suggest Griffen! Great pediatrician, but not partner material." He pursed his lips, then crossed his arms. "I bet she was messing with McSteamy and—" The words died as he looked at Wren.

"And?"

Color was rushing up Seth's neck. There was so much hanging on that cutoff sentence. "Nothing." The word sounded like it caught in Seth's throat on the way out.

"Why would she mess with Luca?" Wren crossed her arms, suddenly very defensive of the man she was still annoyed with.

Seth took a deep breath. "Because he is finally talking."

Wren raised an eyebrow.

"To you, at least. You're the first person I've seen get more than a handful of words out of him. He's great with patients, talkative with them, caring, but with colleagues?" Seth shrugged. "The man is a black box."

Wren didn't know what to say to that. "We're old friends."

"Yeah. I've said that before." Seth chuckled. "Now Therese is pregnant, and we're living in my tiny apartment. The little family I wasn't even able to dream of."

"Tiny apartment?" Wren didn't want to explore the happily-ever-after Therese and Seth had found. She was glad the two seemed so happy. But Luca didn't have any interest in following that same path.

And I do.

Another certainty she didn't want to address right now.

"Oh, yeah. She couldn't find a place when she moved here and then..." his cheeks darkened "...with the baby, it makes sense for us to be together. Plus, I want her with me, always."

It was cute. The man was so in love. "My building has some two bedrooms available. I know because the manager tried very hard to get me to sign a lease for one of them. I'll send you and Therese the information."

"Thanks."

Wren clicked the images off the screen. "All yours, Dr. Graham. Thanks for pointing out the issue. Saved me time." Then she walked out before he could say anything else.

She had the information she needed for Charlie's consult. Not the best news. They'd need to do another surgery. Something no patient enjoyed hearing.

"I said get the hell out!" The clattering sound of something hitting the wall came from Eddie Jenkin's room, and Wren took off without thinking.

Eddie's life was the definition of hell right now. A car accident two weeks ago had destroyed everything he thought he had. He was the patient who had burns over forty percent of his body and the fiancée who'd informed him the moment he'd woken from surgery that she didn't want to stand by him in the situation. The man's long road to recovery was getting no help from his attitude.

Luca was in the corner, his hands up. "Don't throw anything else." The words came up as he saw her walk in, and a frown immediately crossed his lips.

Protection mode.

It seemed that was the role Luca was most prone to stepping into. She replayed those moments she'd thought they might kiss, and he—well, that was not the problem for right now.

"Eddie." Wren kept her voice low but made sure it was clear she expected him to listen.

"I don't want to hear it, Doc. I don't care if I will get *mostly* better." Eddie glared at his chest, still covered with bandages to help with the infection he'd gotten. "Will the scars disappear? Will it bring Beth back? Will my life be exactly like it was?"

"No." She always made sure she was honest with her patients. Eddie's life was forever changed. Though she personally thought he was better off without Beth. If the woman bailed before she ever took her vows, then that meant she wasn't cut out to spend the rest of her life abiding by the *in sickness and health* part.

Eddie closed his eyes, water leaking from them.

"But you will have a life," Luca added from the corner.

"Some life."

"It is what you make of it. Do you know how many families wish they had the chance to bring a loved one back? How many people would beg for a do-over for someone who left this mortal plane?" Luca's voice cracked.

Wren looked at him. The emotion in his face

broke her heart. Who was he speaking of? Ronan? A person who'd entered his life in the decade they'd lost touch?

"I would take their place in a heartbeat."

"No, you wouldn't, Eddie." Luca walked over to the bed and sat on the edge of it. "You didn't deserve this. And you certainly have the right to be angry, scared and hurt. But if you only let yourself feel those emotions, you will miss out on the hope, joy and love that life has to offer."

Eddie opened his eyes and shook his head. "Who is going to love this?"

"Someone worthy," Wren offered. "You have an entire life left to live. The answer is someone worthy."

"Exactly as Dr. Freson says. Now let her take a look at the wounds because the simple stretch I was showing you should not hurt as much as it did." Luca crossed his arms and nodded to Eddie. "I suspect you're in more pain than you're telling anyone."

Wren stepped to the bed. "Is that true?" She looked at the wet bandages.

Eddie bit his lip. "My body was literally roasted in the car accident. I am always in pain. My dad was an opioid addict. Started after he broke a leg." He started to cross his arms and flinched.

"I understand your concern about addiction issues." It was actually a good sign. A man intent on not caring about himself didn't worry about such things. "But we have to let your body heal. I am going to take the wet bandages off."

His patient record indicated that he didn't always let the nurses do their checks. He was just skirting the line of asking to leave against medical advice.

And Wren suspected that, if he could take care of himself, he would do exactly that.

He didn't fight her, whether because he wanted help or because he was too mentally exhausted, she wasn't sure. And it didn't matter.

It took all her years of training not to gasp at the red streaks snaking up his chest. She saw Luca's eyes widen out of the corner of her eye, but he held his tongue.

This was a moment she hated having with patients. There was no sugarcoating this. No sunshiny way to make it better. He was killing himself by not letting the staff help him.

"I need you to make a choice, Eddie." Her voice was firm, and his gaze was rooted on hers. "You've told more than one nurse here to leave when they needed to change your dressing. Thrown things to make them leave."

His eyes filled with tears, but he didn't interrupt.

"You are an adult. Mentally competent. Which means they have to abide by your wishes. So you need to choose. Are you going to fight for the life you can live? A beautiful life story that you can write however you want."

"Or?" The squeaked-out word was barely audible.

"Or the infection crawling up your chest will almost certainly go to your heart. Weaken it and shorten that life story. You get to decide. But the moment to decide is now. Because I need to start an aggressive form of treatment in the next hour."

It was not hyperbole. He needed intravenous antibiotics stat. And she'd make sure to alert cardio that their expertise might be needed. If the infection hit his heart—

That was a problem for the future. One they could hopefully avoid.

Eddie looked at his chest for several beats, clearly weighing his options. "Antibiotics. I don't want to die."

"I am glad to hear that. We are going to start now. But from this moment on, every nurse that walks in here, you let them do the work they need to do. You do not have to do it with a smile, but you will let them do it and be polite."

Luca shifted beside her but didn't add anything to the commentary. This was her show. Her patient.

"I am putting in the orders now. If you refuse again, I will instruct the nurses to give you the Against Medical Advice paperwork." She clicked a few buttons on the tablet, making sure it was notified as stat. And a note to cardio to make sure they understood Eddie might need their services. "I will check on you tomorrow. And I will stop to get a report from the nurses station first." Wren waited a minute, but it was clear that Eddie had exhausted his word bank for now. She'd make sure the staff psychologist saw him, and maybe the chaplain.

He needed to find someone to talk to about the anger clawing through him.

She stepped out and knew Luca was behind her. A nurse was headed toward the room, a bag of antibiotics in her hand.

"If he gives you trouble, give him AMA paperwork." The nurse's eyes widened at Wren's words. "But I think he's pretty docile right now."

The nurse took a deep breath, then headed into the room.

Luca tilted his head and, after a moment, smiled. "I don't hear anything crashing."

Wren nodded, exhaustion hitting her hard. "Thank you for talking him down."

"I never thought I'd play good cop while you, the sunniest person in this hospital, played the bad guy."

It wasn't a role she liked, but there were times it was necessary. "He needed to know."

"And you handled it brilliantly, Wren."

"Thank you. If you don't mind, I'm going to call a rain check on pho." She needed a night to figure out what she wanted to do. A night to plan out a way to make sure the crush she'd developed on the man before her stayed controlled in its little box.

He pushed a hand through his dark hair. "Listen, about Therese—"

"I have a patient. I am running behind. Thanks for your help, Luca." She started down the hall and made sure she didn't look back. The encounter with Eddie had stolen all the air from her.

She needed time. And maybe to put some distance between the friendship that had developed so easily between her and Luca.

CHAPTER EIGHT

WREN STOOD IN the kitchen trying to force herself to make dinner. Or use her phone to order delivery. It was such a simple choice.

And I am frozen.

She wrapped her arms around herself and tried to take deep breaths like her therapist in college had instructed. *Executive freeze* was the term he'd used over and over again.

Wren didn't have attention deficit disorder, which was where the term was most often used. Still, her therapist insisted that her occasional inability to make decisions after rough days and high stress was the same. It was her always-on brain finally shutting itself off for a change.

Her parents had insisted that she was being dramatic.

It's just dinner.

Tears flooded her eyes. This wasn't worth crying over. But she couldn't stop them.

Her stomach grumbled, adding its voice to the conversation but no helpful notes for her brain. If she hadn't canceled her dinner date with Luca, she'd have at least had pho and chocolate cake ready to go.

It wasn't a date. And that was why she'd canceled. Because her brain couldn't make her heart understand that. And now she was frozen over a dumb food decision.

Pick something. Pick something. Pick something.

The repetitive mental scream did nothing but send more tears racing down her face. She'd burned all her energy giving Eddie his options and avoiding Therese and Luca for the rest of her shift.

Avoiding them hadn't made her mind stop twisting through scenarios where she mentally replayed ways to tell Therese she actually was interested in dating. None of them worked.

Why did I say I don't date?

Those words had just popped out. Not a complete lie but not helpful, either. Walking them back would be embarrassing. Particularly because she was interested in dating...just not any of Therese's selectees. And then add all that to what Seth said about Therese ribbing Luca.

Luca.

Wren's head overflowed with of thoughts of him. An acknowledgment that the friendly nights they'd spent together meant far more to her than to him. So many thoughts that her brain refused to process one more.

A knock at the door.

Wren spun, well aware there was only one person who could be standing on the other side of that barrier.

Now there were three options flooding her brain. Dinner. Leaving the knock unanswered. Letting

Luca in. Her feet didn't move. If she stayed frozen, option two was going to win by default.

"I know you're in there, Wren. I have a surprise."

She brushed the tears off her cheeks, fully aware there was no hiding the fact that she'd spent far too long crying. Over something she'd heard time and time again growing up was "no big deal."

Another knock, then her phone buzzed.

You out? I have a surprise.

She swallowed and stepped to the door. The look on his face as he met her gaze was confirmation enough that she looked terrible.

The stuffed mermaid doll in his hands fell to the floor. "What's wrong?"

"Nothing. Everything's fine." She ran a hand along her neck, very aware that the squeak in her voice made it clear that everything was, in fact, not fine.

"Wren." Luca bent down to grab the surprise, then stepped into the apartment. "You're crying."

She stepped back to let him close the door.

The tears were still coming. "I never cry." She gestured to the offending wet streaks. "Because when I do, I can't turn them off. Not great company tonight, Luca."

"You don't need to be great company. Why are you sobbing?"

She laughed, but the sound held no mirth. "I can't figure out what I want for dinner."

"Dinner?"

"Yep." She shrugged and barely caught the second laugh bubbling in her throat. She was dangerously close to losing it even more. "My parents used to call this my crazy brain. Not a nice term."

"I'd say it's pretty freaking derogatory." His hand found hers, and she didn't like the way her heart sighed and her brain calmed just a bit.

"Executive freeze. I guess I overdid it today and—" Her mind had no follow-up, so the *and* just dangled in the air, waiting for a completion her brain had no ability to offer.

"I want pizza," Luca said suddenly. "I was actually getting ready to order a pie. How about I order us a large pepperoni with pineapple and black olives?"

Not her first choice of pizza, but if he was taking the lead, she could pick the pineapple off. "Sounds good."

"No. It doesn't." He squeezed her hand, a reminder that she hadn't pulled away.

Neither has he.

Luca pulled her into a hug, and her body ached to collapse into him. "Okay. That was my bad. I figured the combination would get a laugh. So this is more serious than I imagined. I will order pepperoni with black olives unless you nod to tell me you want the pineapple, which I will get, but I will be putting all the pineapple on your pieces."

"No!" She shook her head against his shoulder. "No pineapple."

His hand ran down her back. "All right. And ice cream. We are ordering ice cream. I want strawberry. I will get a tub of chocolate, vanilla, and rocky road."

"I can't eat all that. Just chocolate. Dark chocolate if they have it." The words came easier this time.

He laid his head against hers. For a moment, she thought his lips had brushed her hair.

They didn't. Right?

"You okay for me to step away and order?"

"Oh." She started to pull back, but his arms didn't release her.

"I asked a question, Wren. Oh is not an answer; it is a response—one that seems like you might be thinking you did something wrong. I will stand here holding you all night if you want."

She wouldn't mind that, but not in the way he meant.

"I am all right." She stepped back. "Thank you."

"Of course." He grinned, his jeweled gaze holding her so close. After a minute, he held up his phone. "Ordering time." His fingers flew across the screen.

Her brain was silent. So calm. She took the first breath that didn't feel like knives running to her lungs in hours.

Luca put his phone away and held up the mermaid stuffed toy he'd laid on the counter by the door. "This is why I'm actually here." He pushed the stuffie toward her. "Is it the right one?"

She looked at it, not wanting to hurt his feelings. "It's nice. How sweet. Thank you."

"It's not the right one. I can tell." He glared at the stuffed toy. "You'll have to show me a picture."

She pressed her hand against his shoulder and started to lean toward him before she caught herself. She was not kissing his cheek. "That movie was more than twenty years old when I saw that stuffed animal. Assuming there are any left, they are with collectors and far too expensive to fulfill a childhood want. This one is perfect."

"Except it isn't the right one."

"Luca." She put her hand on his chest. He leaned toward her, and even after forcing herself to pull back seconds ago, she leaned in and kissed his cheek. The platonic kiss was over in milliseconds, but that didn't stop her lips from burning. "Thank you."

Her brain was quiet. Her heart rate level. Because Luca was here. She didn't feel like investigating that too closely right now.

He frowned. "I got the wrong one. The online shop said it was an original."

He'd gone looking for her. A present just for her. It didn't matter if it was "wrong." It was the best gift she'd ever gotten. She pressed the stuffed toy to her chest. "You searched for something for me. Just me. I can't explain how much that means."

His phone dinged. "Delivery's here. I am going to run grab it."

"And get Hippo, too. Don't want the poor boy to get lonely."

* * *

"I'm getting another piece, you want one?" Wren popped off the couch, a lot happier than she'd been when he arrived.

His sunshiny Wren was wrecked, and he'd nearly panicked when she answered the door. The tears, the frustration—he'd wanted to wipe away whatever caused the issue.

She's not mine.

It was getting harder and harder to remember that. This was friendship. It was easy. She was a person who only saw him for himself.

Because she doesn't know about the money.

The inside of his cheek stung as he forced his teeth to unlock. Wren wouldn't care.

Probably.

That was the problem. He'd hadn't expected Madeline to care. Or his parents. Or his friends.

And each one had lost sight of Luca and focused on the wallet they coveted. He never got to go back to the Luca they cared about once people knew. He couldn't lose Wren. He just couldn't.

"Earth to Luca! Do you want me to bring another piece?"

"I am quite full." His cheeks heated as he rubbed his belly. Hippo let out a sound that indicated he'd be more than happy if a piece landed on the bed Wren bought, and Luca laughed.

Maybe that was a warning sign that he and Hippo were here too often, but it wasn't one he planned to listen to. At least not tonight.

"You had *a* piece, Luca. One small piece. You don't really expect me to believe you are full. Pu—leee—ase!"

He held up a hand, grinning. Might as well let the cat out of the bag. "Don't get mad."

She tilted her head. "I am making no promises." But the grin on her face relaxed him.

"I ate before I stopped down. I had some leftovers and chowed down on them in my kitchen."

"Over the sink?" She giggled and slid two more slices onto her plate.

"I could lie." He'd made a joke about his eating habit last week. That if no one was around he ate in the kitchen, usually over the sink.

She'd "lovingly" reminded him that he was always alone—at least until she forced her way into his life. A truth he didn't care to look at too closely.

"Why don't you date?" The question was out, and sirens were echoing in his head. He wanted to know. Hell, he'd planned to ask, though every script he'd started was more like the monologue of a bad made-for-TV movie than the last.

Each of those would still have been better than blurting the question out into the open.

Wren took two bites of her pizza, then set the plate in her lap. "Why are you asking?"

Her dark gaze glittered as she stared at him across the couch. Less than two feet separated them. Two feet and a gulf of indecision. The answer to this question meant something. But he had no idea what.

"You said it almost in a hurt way today. Like a wound."

She frowned but didn't say anything.

"I don't want you alone, if that isn't what you want." Almost the truth.

"Right. Protecting me. I don't need you doing that, Luca."

His responses to Therese today had everything to do with jealousy. The idea of Wren with someone else burned. It wasn't fair to her, but it didn't change his reaction.

"I do date. Sort of." She pushed the plate off her lap, putting it on the coffee table.

Hippo opened an eye, raised his snout and let out a huff as Luca motioned for him to stay on the bed.

"Sort of? What does that mean?" He started to reach for her hand but pulled back.

Her dark gaze floated to his hand. "I am the odd gal out. I had friends in New York, but while they were falling in love and juggling med school, relationships, sometimes new babies, I was celebrating my sweet sixteen. Or my twenty-first birthday after they'd been legal drinkers for years."

"Always a little apart." That was a feeling Luca understood. One he hated that they had in common.

"Right."

"Okay, but now you're twenty-six. So the age barrier—"

"Twenty-six, and I've kissed exactly three people in my life." Her hand flew over her mouth, her eyes wide as the secret hovered in the short distance between them.

"So inexperienced?" Luca knew he wasn't hiding the shock on his face. She was perfection. Wren should be beating would-be-suitors away.

"Virginal. Happy? There, I said it." Her bottom lip popped out as she pointed at him. "That face. That face right there is why I don't tell anyone. Particularly men."

Luca held up a hand. "Sorry. I'm just stunned."

"Yeah, well, twelve-year-old college student, sixteen-year-old med student and plastics resident at nineteen meant the only people interested in me were criminals and creeps. And now—"

She took a deep breath, crossed her legs and wrapped her arms tightly around herself. Pulling herself together. Protecting herself.

He'd answered wrong. The gulf widened, and he wasn't sure how to string a rope across the roaring tides. The sunny demeanor was something people might think was a weakness. But there was steel coursing through Wren's veins.

"And now?" he pressed as he mentally tried to figure out how to dig out of the hole he'd dug. Something he always seemed to do with this incredible woman.

"And now…" Wren looked over his shoulder, out the window. "I am either seen as too much work or a prize to be won. A coveted object."

Object.

Luca didn't have any words for that horrific revelation.

"Why are you so concerned with it?" Wren lifted her chin. "I was very specific that I didn't want you stepping into a brotherly role."

"That is *very* much not the role I am trying to claim." The husky words poured forth, and he watched Wren's eyes widen.

Before he could process what was happening, she was in his lap, lips against his, arms around his neck.

Luca's arms wrapped around her waist, pulling her closer. Whatever this was, he wasn't thinking. Wasn't second-guessing. There was no one in the world but him and Wren; nothing but this moment.

Her hands slid down his cheeks as she pulled back. "Luca—"

He leaned forward, capturing whatever words were destined to flow from her sweet lips. Her mouth opened, and he took full advantage. She tasted warm and spicy.

His hands wrapped through her dark hair, pulling her closer—though that shouldn't be possible.

"Luca." This time his name sounded like a prayer on her soft lips.

Wren's hands went to the edge of his shirt, hesitating for only a moment before slipping under. The subtle touch of her fingers on his belly was fire, a flame darting under each movement.

His lips trailed along her chin, reining in his own desire. Tonight was Wren's. Only Wren's. Wrapping his arms tightly around her waist, he flipped them. Now it was her leaning against the back of the couch cushion.

Her bright eyes held his as his fingers trailed up her toned legs, slowing on her inner thigh. Wren's breath caught and her head fell back.

He took complete advantage of her exposed neck, nipping kisses along it until he got to the top of her collarbone. Her pert nipples were straining against the light pink tank top, confirming what he'd suspected. That cotton top was the only thing between him and her perky breasts.

Letting his thumb wander to the top of the loose black running shorts she wore, he stared at her. Wren's dark gaze glittered with need—for him.

Wren's hips pressed against his, and he watched the awareness of his need register in her eyes. Her hand started to slip between them, but he grabbed it, kissing the tip of each finger before placing it over her head. His erection pressed against his pants, demanding in a way he'd never known.

Wren's hips molded against him as she pulled his shirt over his head.

"You are so beautiful." Her fingers danced across his shoulders.

"That is supposed to be my line." Luca let his hand roam the edge of her tank top, need coursing through his body. "Can I take your top off?"

Heat coated her cheeks, but she nodded and adjusted her position, just a little, to make it easier for him. *Damn.*

He placed the shirt on the back of the couch within easy reach, if she wanted it.

Running a thumb along the edge of one perky nipple, Luca bent his head, feathering kisses along her lips. Slowly, he slid his mouth down her throat and chest before finally capturing one nipple. He stroked it with his tongue, enjoying each tiny moan slipping from Wren's lips.

"Luca." The pant coming after his name sent shivers down his spine.

"Wren," he breathed as he slid his mouth across her chest and started worshiping her other nipple.

"I burn."

"Mmm." No woman had ever said such a thing in his arms. He slid a free hand up her thigh. "Where do you burn, Wren?"

He lifted his head, watching color crest from her perfect breasts to her cheeks. She writhed under him, forcing his hand farther up her thigh.

"Where, honey?" Luca wanted her to say it. Wanted to hear the words from her sweet lips.

"Between my legs." She didn't look away as she said it. "I ache."

"That is a problem I can fix." He returned his lips to her chest as the hand on her thigh flew higher, darting to the inside of her shorts. Cotton panties greeted him. Letting his thumb sweep against her mound, he lifted his head.

By her own admission, no man had ever touched her this way. He was going to watch the orgasm crest across her features.

"Luca, mmm." Her hips undulated against the caress. "It's…it's…not enough."

Each caught breath anchored him.

Pulling her panties to the side, he pressed his thumb to her nub and grinned as her back arched. "That's right, Wren." Keeping the pressure on her, he slipped a finger into her heat.

She bit her lip, surging against him, need clearly driving her. Luca didn't change anything, he let her control her body, using him as the tool to get what she craved.

Perfection. That was what this moment was.

"Luca."

His name echoing around them as she orgasmed was spellbinding. As her body relaxed, he pulled his finger from her and slid it across his lips. "You taste magnificent."

Wren's glazed gaze captured him as she pressed on his shoulders, sliding into his lap. "I think it's your turn."

"No." He caught the argument he knew was brewing. "Tonight…" he kissed her "…was just about…" his lips dragged across her, as her hips danced on his erection "…you."

"Tomorrow?" Her finger floated along the edge of his pants zipper. His pants were already damp with precum, and the feel of her hand through the denim was nearly enough to bring him to completion.

"Tomorrow." He brushed his lips against her. "Tomorrow."

CHAPTER NINE

WREN LOOKED OVER the notes in Eddie's chart. He'd let the nursing staff change his bandages. He'd refused pain meds but was taking the antibiotic treatment. A win.

"Morning, sunshine." Luca grinned as he stepped next to her.

Her body heated with the memories of his lips on hers. His fingers. His touch. She'd acted rashly. He'd nearly growled that his interest wasn't brotherly, and after the long day her impulse control was apparently shot.

Thank goodness.

"McSteamy." She raised her chin and winked at him.

He leaned a little closer, not touching, but his breath was warm on her ear. "I've never minded the nickname, but I might actually like it from your lips."

Any words she had were stuck in the back of her throat.

"I am headed in to see Eddie." Luca tilted his head toward the door as he raised his hand in a wave. "Multiple nurses are staring."

"Well, you *are* hovering." Wren tucked the tablet under her arm. She didn't turn to look at the nurses station, knowing her cheeks were already stained with heat.

Tonight. The promised word. She had to get through today, and then tonight.

Focus.

"I need to see to Eddie, too. Why are you headed that way?" Eddie needed physical therapy. A lot of it. But right now, the infection was the top priority.

"He is so angry." Luca let out a sigh, the playboy attitude disappearing as he shifted to physical therapist mode.

"His fiancée left him because he was in an accident. Even if his road to recovery was easier, that would send most people for a loop." She'd watched the woman take the ring off, and fury had rippled through her. And Eddie was a stranger. The man had a right to be angry. But it could also destroy him. A delicate balance.

"I know. But I have been there."

Madeline. How had Wren forgotten her? She'd sat in the front row, making faces at her brother from the groom's side until Luca had raced out and pulled him to the side. It was Ronan who announced the groom was leaving.

"I thought you left her at the altar." The words slid out. If there weren't people in the hallway passing by, she'd let out a curse. "Sorry."

"Water under the bridge." His shoulders were tight, but his jaw was relaxed. "I did. Sort of. I overheard her talking in the bridal suite. Came to surprise her, and well, let's just say I heard more than she intended."

Maybe it didn't matter what he'd heard more than a decade ago, but Wren's brain was running through a list of possible reasons anyway, given that he didn't seem interested in elaborating.

"I was angry for a long time. Furious." He let out a breath that she was pretty sure he didn't realize he'd held onto.

"How long?" Was the aborted wedding the reason his colleagues didn't know him? The reason that, until she came along, he ate over the sink in his supersized apartment?

"What?" Luca looked at her.

He'd heard her. But if he didn't want to answer, she wasn't going to push. Particularly because they'd reached the door of Eddie's room.

"Doc." Eddie nodded to Wren. "Torture artist." He didn't offer a smile to Luca, but he looked more relaxed than he had yesterday.

"I can see you've accepted all the treatments from the nurses. With grace even." Wren set the tablet on the counter. "How are you feeling?"

"Like burned meat. But the pain is less." Eddie caught himself as he started to shrug. "I still don't feel like myself."

"That makes sense." Wren had requested a counselor appointment for him, but that request was still pending. Hopefully this afternoon, someone would be here.

"I used to be happy. All the time. People used

to joke that a party never really started until I got there. The life of the party." Eddie rolled his eyes. "I hate this version of myself."

Wren laid a hand on the tiny unburned portion of his shoulder. "You can get that person back."

"Why is the torture artist here?" Eddie glared at Luca, and Wren thought there was a decent chance the glare was serious. Shifting topics was fine, but she'd make sure to elevate the request for a counselor.

"Because you need to do some stretches. Little ones. And to talk." Luca sidled up to the other side of the bed.

"What do you want to talk about?" Eddie narrowed his eyes. "New ways to make my burned body scream?"

"No, but if you do the stretches I recommended, your healing will speed up. I…" Luca took a deep breath, his gaze shifting to Wren for just a second before focusing on Eddie. "My fiancée told her maid of honor she couldn't imagine spending forever with me. But she planned to hang out for a few years. Get some advantages of married life, then leave me in the dust." Luca crossed his arms.

At least Luca was too focused on Eddie to realize what that revelation was doing to Wren. She'd met Madeline a few times, never gotten on with her. Which was expected. After all, they were nearly a decade apart in age. But now she wanted to throttle the woman.

Eddie raised his arms to let Wren look at the

wet bandages, but his gaze didn't leave Luca. The wounds were less angry today. He'd set his healing back at least two weeks, but hopefully they'd turned a corner.

"Beth left me because of an accident. Why did yours leave you?"

"Same reason yours left you." Luca pulled a stress ball from the bag he carried to all the rooms he visited. "She didn't love me. Just the idea of me. Or the idea of a wedding."

Wren risked a look at Luca; his gaze was rooted on Eddie. Either Eddie didn't realize Luca hadn't given an answer, not really, or he didn't want to push. It made sense. Luca was helping, but he didn't really know Eddie.

But will he give me the full answer? Wren wasn't sure.

"Either way, you got lucky." Luca looked at Wren, the easiness in his gaze halting her worry. "She outed herself before you put in all the down payments on venues. Before the divorce attorney had to get involved."

"Doesn't feel very lucky." Eddie turned his attention to Wren. "Am I looking better, Doc?"

"You've had twelve hours of intravenous antibiotics. That is not a lot of time, but I am no longer as concerned about the infection getting to your heart."

Luca offered a grin. "That is doctor speak for better but still a long way to go."

Eddie chuckled, then paused, like he was shocked

·the sound had come from him. "I didn't realize torture artists were also doctor translators."

"They serve many roles." Wren put the wet bandage back over the wound. "Ideally, we'd be getting you ready for skin grafts, but with the infection, surgery will need to be pushed."

Again. *Ideally*, they'd have done grafts last week. But the uncooperative patient had made that impossible. Eddie looked away, color creeping along his neck. Hopefully he was turning a corner in accepting care.

"I'll be back to check on you tomorrow."

"And I am going to go over some stretches you can do in this bed," Luca said. "And we can talk, if you want."

"I don't." Eddie pinched his eyes closed as she headed for the door. "How long until you found someone to spend your life with after your fiancée destroyed everything?"

Wren's hand stilled on the room's door, her ears pricking to hear the answer.

"Still working on that. But let's just say there are some glimmers on the horizon."

Glimmers on the horizon. Tonight. The promise burned in her belly.

Stepping into the hall, she saw Therese coming out of one of the other rooms. "Therese."

The woman's cheeks filled with pink as she stepped toward Wren. "Wren. I want to apologize again. Seth told me how uncomfortable I made you.

Not that I hadn't picked that up on my own. I was giving Luca a hard time and—"

"Thank you." Wren hadn't gotten Therese's attention to talk about Luca, but she was sure that without being at her wit's end, she would never have jumped into his arms last night. And if she hadn't done that, she doubted she'd be spending today looking forward to tonight's encore.

Therese's eyes widened. "Oh my gosh." She clapped her hands. "I knew it. I am going to make sure Seth knows that forcing the issue didn't completely blow up in my face." She let out a sigh.

"I didn't call you over for that revelation." Wren pulled a brochure out of the deep pocket of her doctor's coat. "I checked, and one of the two-bedroom apartments I told Seth about is still available. If you mention that you know me and Luca, the approval process should speed up quickly."

Therese looked at the brochure.

"Seth mentioned the tiny apartment, and with the little one coming—" Wren waited a second, concern building as Therese's eyes looked like they were filling with tears. "I hope I didn't overstep."

Therese waved a hand. "Hormones. I cry at the drop of a hat these days. And, I mean, I overstepped yesterday. Just because it worked out doesn't change that truth. So I know what overstepping is, and this is not it. The building looks nice, I'll have Seth make the call. I suspect hearing from a well-established plastic surgeon will hold a little more weight than me and my less than stellar credit. I couldn't find a single place when I first moved here. Though, that ended up working out." She grinned as she ran a hand over her little baby bump.

It had indeed.

"Let me know if you need a reference. Though Luca is probably the better reference. I have almost a month under my rent belt, but he owns his apartment."

Therese's eyes widened. So it wasn't just Wren that thought that was beyond impressive. "Wow."

"Yeah. Maybe Seth should mention Luca." Wren grinned. "I need to finish rounds. But thank you, Therese."

"You're welcome."

Luca started to light the candles on the dining room table, then held off as he looked at his watch. Wren was always punctual. There were still three minutes before she was due up here.

Three minutes that feels like three hours.

If she wasn't hungry for dinner, he didn't want to have to come back here to blow out candles when he could be spending important time exploring her body.

Luca rocked back on his heels and did not check his watch again. Time was moving but not fast enough. The whole day had seemed that way.

He'd checked back in on Eddie just before leaving. He was doing his exercises. Grumpy but moving. Luca was taking the win.

But the words he'd uttered this morning had struck Luca's soul. *I hate this version of myself.*

Luca had encased himself in an armor he'd never intended to wear. Formed the day Madeline said she was only marrying him for money, hardened by his parents that only called when they needed a favor and sealed when his best friend passed away in the car he'd help secure for him.

Wren had loosened the steel around his heart. Made him feel like himself, feel whole. A man he hadn't realized he was missing until she'd beamed into his orbit. He hoped Ronan's spirit didn't mind. The idea that he'd never get to ask bothered him, but it was a tiny squeak in the back of his mind now rather than a bleating alarm.

Hippo started for the door, his little toe dance making it obvious he'd picked up on Wren's footsteps before she reached the door.

Luca followed, not dancing, but his soul was certainly celebrating. He ripped the door open, grinning as Wren's hand, poised for knocking, stilled.

"Were you staring out the peephole waiting for me?"

Luca grabbed her hand, pulling her in. She wore a black lacy sheath dress that made his mouth water. The freedom to touch her…to drop a light kiss on her lips… He finally understood the definition of exhilarating.

"I have my own alarm system." Luca nodded to Hippo. "I mean, he's actually a terrible alarm system." The dog thought everyone in the world was a friend. "But his hearing is excellent."

Wren bent down and gave the gray pittie a pat. She didn't release Luca's hand, though.

"I've got pasta and a cookie cake." Luca grinned. "Hungry?"

Wren bit her lip. "I might have had a snack before coming up. But if you're hungry."

Luca snapped his fingers three times, and Hippo started for his bed. He didn't want the dog underfoot for this next part. "I am starving." He lifted her off her feet, enjoying her squeal and the feel of her arms wrapping around his neck. "But dinner can certainly wait."

"Luca." Wren's lips pressed against his neck, light kisses that sent bolts of desire flowing through him.

"I do like the way you say my name." He kicked the bedroom door shut as he took her to the bed.

"I say it normal." Wren popped up on her knees and lifted his shirt with ease.

There was a frenzied energy about her. That was not what tonight was about. "Wren."

"Don't look at me like that."

He lifted her chin, making sure she was looking at him. "I am a drowning man, honey. I have never needed someone as much as I need you." He grabbed her hand before it could reach the button of his slacks. "But we are not rushing this. Anticipation has coated my skin all day. And I plan to make you beg with need." His fingers danced along the edge of the lacy dress. "You should wear this out sometime. It is absolutely gorgeous." He slipped his hand underneath her, cupping her tight ass, enjoying the hitch in her breath as she pulled closer to him.

"I'm glad you like it." Color shot up her neck, and he dropped his head, dragging his lips along her neck.

"I loved the tank top and shorts last night, and this outfit is mouthwatering. But my favorite is…" he slid his hand up her thigh "…nothing at all." He lifted the dress over her hips. "Raise your hands, honey."

She did as he instructed, and he stripped it from her lithe body.

Tonight she wore a black thong, a matching piece to the slinky dress. Gorgeous, and another night, he'd beg her to wear this combo and spend hours out on the town with him, knowing the perfection waiting for him when they got back home. But tonight, he needed her naked, beneath him, panting his name.

Hooking his fingers through the material, he pulled the thong down her thighs and threw it on the floor. "Naked," he breathed and captured her mouth. His thumb danced along one breast and then the other.

Wren's hand ran through his hair as he lowered his attentions to her breasts. Suckling each as his fingers skimmed her upper thigh.

Slowly, ever so slowly, his mouth moved lower. He felt her still, and then gasp as his tongue darted along her bud.

"Luca." Wren gripped the bedsheets as his tongue darted across her slit.

"You taste magnificent. I got a taste last night but…" He drove his tongue into her heat, loving the moans echoing above him.

"Luca…" This time his name was a pant on her lips. "Luca, please."

The plea nearly broke him, but he wasn't joining them until she'd come for him at least once.

Replacing his tongue with a finger, he returned his mouth's attention to her breasts. She was spiraling, so close to the edge.

When the moment came, it was his name on her lips.

"Wren." His mouth captured hers as he quickly undid his pants and kicked them and his boxers off.

Her hand darted to his length, and her long fingers stroking him was maddening. Luca grabbed a condom from his nightstand, sheathed himself, then pressed against her core.

Wren's dark gaze held his, and he heard the gasp as he joined them together. His lips were on hers, as he held himself, letting her adjust to his length.

"Luca?" This time his name was much less certain on her sweet lips.

"Yes?"

Her hips shifted a little, the motion screaming through his body.

"I don't have any experience, but…is this all?" She bit her lip.

His Wren.

"Not at all." He slipped a hand between them, rubbing her swollen nub as he moved. Her motions were uncertain at first, but then her rhythm matched his.

"Luca." Her arms were wrapped around his shoulders, her feet interlocked on his back, driving him ever closer to the edge.

When he finally crested, she held him, kissing his cheek. Their hearts beating seemingly in time.

CHAPTER TEN

WREN RAN HER hand along Luca's chest, enjoying the quiet blend of his breaths with Hippo's snores. She'd never slept in anyone's arms. Never felt the heat of another's body next to her. It was oddly satisfying.

Her hand dipped lower, and his manhood jolted. She grinned. The idea that so little from her turned him on was quite thrilling. She was still sore from last night, but also wildly curious. He'd been in control.

A fact she didn't mind, but she'd touched him so little compared to the bliss he'd given her.

Her fingers wrapped around the hard length, and she knew from the change in his breathing that Luca was very much awake. "Do you want me to stop?"

He shook his head against the pillow, his eyes flying open to look at her. "Wren."

She could see why he liked how she said his name when he was tormenting her with pleasure. Such a satisfying sound.

Wren dropped a light kiss on his lips as she continued her slow strokes along his length. The man was literal putty in her hands. Intoxicating.

Moving along his body, she pressed kisses to his chest, his abs, his hips and then just above his manhood. One of his hands trailed along her thigh, the other ran through her hair. No pressure, no demands.

Her core ignited as she took him in her mouth. Licking the tip of his erection, she enjoyed the shift in his position as she pleasured him.

"Wren." His hips bucked, and he pulled her head off him just before he came. "You are going to be the end of me." His mouth covered hers before she could think of anything to say.

"What do you say we grab a shower and then figure out a plan for the day?" he asked.

"Plan?"

His jade gaze rooted to hers, a look there she wasn't able to decipher. "We have the day off. I assumed you'd want to spend it together."

"Yeah. I need to get clothes and eat and—"

"Shower with me, Wren. We will plan all of it out after a shower, breakfast and coffee." Luca grabbed her hand, slid off the bed and moved them swiftly to the bathroom.

Wren smiled as she headed back up to Luca's apartment. They were heading to the aquarium after taking Hippo for a walk. The entire day. Just the two of them.

Her phone buzzed, and she pulled it out of her pocket.

Talked to the apartment complex.

Told them we knew Luca. It got a little weird.

Weird? What could that mean?

Weird how?

It was standard to list tenants you knew. There was space on the form she'd filled out. Of course, Wren had left hers blank.

Wren pinched the bridge of her nose. Of course. Luca wasn't a tenant. The idea of him owning his whole floor seemed so out of place she hadn't thought of it when suggesting Therese and Seth list him. He had lived here longer, but the rental agency didn't deal with him.

Ugh. It's because Luca owns his place. I shouldn't have recommended putting him down. I didn't really think about it.

The elevator opened, and she stepped onto his floor but didn't move toward his door. She hesitated over the call button, then pressed it. Better to figure this out through actually talking than back-and-forth texts.

Therese answered on the first ring. "Hey, Wren. I was trying to figure out how to answer the weird question. Glad you called."

"Guess owning the apartment means he isn't a tenant. Duh. The idea is just so foreign to me."

Therese laughed. "Fair. I mean who owns an apartment in this city? Seth is one of the top plastic surgeons in San Diego, well established in his career, and even he is renting. Man. Good for Luca, but yeah, we should have considered he wasn't a tenant, too."

The laugh was happy but the words after it sent a tiny warning bubble through her belly. It was odd. And he didn't own an apartment. He owned the penthouse floor. The entire top of the building was his.

An investment hit. That made sense, but it also wasn't an in-depth answer. And she hadn't dug any further.

Just like she hadn't dug any further on the reasons Madeline had wanted to stick around for a while but not forever.

"The renting agent asked how I knew Dr. McDonnell. Pressed pretty hard actually. I don't know. We just listed his name. And Luca mentioned the place to Seth, so I thought… I don't know. Ugh. I keep saying that. It was a vibe thing. I know that sounds dumb."

A vibe thing. There was no answer in that.

"It seemed like they were asking if we were looking for a discount because we knew him." Therese's sigh was heavy on the other side of the phone. "I mean, usually it's the tenant making money from the referral, not the renter, right?"

"Right." The rental form had indicated that if she referred a tenant who signed a one-year lease she got two hundred dollars off a month's rent. Not much, but it was fairly standard in the city.

"Seth is wondering if he should check with Luca or if we should just look elsewhere."

"I'm actually a few feet from his apartment. I'll check and text, okay?" Wren looked toward Luca's door and bit her lip. This wasn't a big deal. But there was that bubble in her stomach again.

"I really want to know more about that." Therese said something to Seth that Wren couldn't make out, then came back to the conversation. "I appreciate you asking about the apartment. And seriously, I want to know more about you being outside his place."

Wren said goodbye and grinned at the phone. It was nice to have a friend that wanted information for fun's sake. Not intelligence questions or medical facts. Just a friend.

Luca's door opened, and he brought Hippo out, already in his harness. "Any reason you're just hanging out in my hall? Hippo has been going nuts for the last few minutes waiting for you to wander down this way."

Wren walked up, kissed his cheek, then bent to pat Hippo on the head. The giant potato didn't seem too bothered by anything. "Was Hippo missing me or was it you?"

Luca pulled her to his side. "Maybe a little of both." His lips pressed against hers. "But also, *why* were you just hanging out here?"

"Talking to Therese. They ran into a little trouble when they put your name on the rental form. Said the rental manager made it seem like they were asking for a discount."

"Were they?"

Wren stepped out of Luca's arms, shocked by the statement. "They listed your name on the rental agreement as a tenant."

"I'm not a tenant." Luca pressed the button on the elevator. The words were almost cold.

What was happening here? "I know. I told Therese that I forgot what you owning your apartment really means."

"You forgot?" Luca stepped into the elevator, and she followed. His gaze held some emotion she couldn't place.

"Your housing is hardly the most interesting thing about you, Luca." She wasn't sure where this conversation had taken such a turn. But discomfort was pouring from him.

"Even the view from the living room?" He raised an eyebrow.

Was he joking? "It's a nice view. Still, not that interesting of a thing. At the end of the day, it's just an apartment." She placed her hand on his chest. Why on earth would his apartment matter to her?

"Right." He shook his head, like he was clearing brain fog or something. "I had someone a few years ago who found out I owned the top floor. They tried to tell the manager they knew me personally and that they were supposed to get an apartment for well below market value."

"Oh. Okay. I'm sure that was frustrating, but Therese said you talked to Seth about this place."

His eyes widened. "I did do that." He slapped his head with a free hand as the door of the elevator opened on the first floor. "And then forgot to tell the rental office. Good grief."

So it had all been a misunderstanding. But it felt like there was more to the story. A bigger reason for the overreaction.

He pulled his phone from his back pocket and swiped his fingers across the screen. "I sent Seth a text. Apologizing and telling him I'd let the front office know."

Wren pulled his free hand into hers. "Why don't we stop by the office, let them know and then take this guy for a pup cup? And get me a…" She put her finger on her lips. "Do I want a cupcake or a fancy coffee?"

Luca beamed, the fog of whatever this conversation was vanishing. "Why not both?"

"Here we are." Luca threw open his car door and ran around to Wren's so he could open it for her.

Wren's hand was warm in his palm.

He'd dated. Not a lot since his aunt's estate closed, but he'd dated. And he'd never felt as excited as he did with Wren. He wasn't sure why the rush felt greater, but he wasn't planning to delve too far into it today. Hearing her say that his apartment wasn't the most interesting thing about him had nearly brought him to his knees before her.

"So the aquarium?" Wren began as they started for the entrance. "I don't know why, but I would never have thought you'd suggest this."

Luca chuckled. "I am a patron of the Birch Aquarium."

"A member. Wow. That I really didn't expect." Wren reached for a map.

"You don't need that." He tapped his head. "I know this place from top to bottom."

Luca had used the right word. He wasn't a member but a patron of the aquarium. He, and some other wealthy families had donated recently to the Living Seas exhibit. It was set to open in just a few weeks. He was on the invite list to the private viewing party just before the public ribbon cutting. He hadn't planned to go, but Wren might enjoy the private exhibit.

"Why do you know the aquarium so well?" Her nose was wrinkled, and her eyes crinkled in surprise.

"Because there are octopuses here. They're off display right now because of the construction, but I have an inside source so we can see if we can get a peek."

He was fascinated by the creatures. They had no bones. No skeleton. His world revolved around muscles, bones and movement. These creatures had structures completely different from humans and moved majestically.

"Octopus. The eight-legged creatures that are the

basis for the mythology of sea monsters?" Wren giggled as he stuck his tongue out.

"It's not their fault that humans saw their magnificence and corrupted it." He let out a playful huff. "Plus, I want to point out that the kraken is most likely based on a giant squid, not an octopus."

Wren squeezed his hand. "My apologies."

He flashed his patron card at the entrance, and the ticket taker let them both through.

"Whoa. You're a member, but I am not. I need to pay—"

The fact that she fully expected to pay her way, with no assumption that he would cover it, was sexy as hell.

Provided he didn't remind himself that she didn't know the depths of his wallet.

"I told you. I'm a patron. Now, you want to see the octopus or the rest of the aquarium first?"

"You are seriously excited to be here." Wren pulled him to a stop at the sea horse exhibit. "Oh my gosh. Look!"

He leaned close to her ear. "I thought you were judging me about my love of octopuses. Did I just discover you love sea horses?"

Wren rolled her eyes. "I don't love them. I like them a lot, though. They are fascinating. I read through a whole set of books on them when I was little." She stepped a little closer to the tank. "I actually thought about going into marine biology. Joked about it several times. My bachelor's degree in microbiology could have led me to multiple graduate programs."

There was a wistfulness to her words. Life was a set of paths taken and missed. It wasn't a bad thing to think about the roads you missed. But there was something in her tone that made him think there was more to it.

"You went to college at eleven. How could you joke about it?" There was something in her tone. A sad acceptance that her life had been scripted?

"Technically, I didn't start until I was twelve." Those words sounded like they should be the punchline of a joke, but there was nothing funny about them.

It took him a minute to finally ask, "So why was marine biology a joke?"

Her parents had been blissfully absent from his and Ronan's lives. At the time, it seemed like he and Ronan could do whatever. Looking back, his parents had just never been interested in him, and Ronan's had felt the same. Through adult eyes, he was able to tell just how messed up that was.

She didn't take her gaze away from the tank. "I mean, it was just accepted that I would go into medicine. And it worked out. The human body is fascinating."

"But you wouldn't have chosen it?"

"I don't know." She shrugged as she watched a sea dragon move in front of them. "I can't imagine being anything other than what I am now. But we are who our parents made us."

The words made him bristle. His parents had all but abandoned him except when they wanted to punish the other. One Christmas he'd gotten the exact same gifts from his mother as he received from his father. All because his father had wanted to upstage his mother by giving him the gifts first.

It was never about Luca.

The only thing he'd gotten from them was Aunt Maude. The woman had loved and cared for him. No questions asked. And made him promise that his parents got nothing.

It wasn't a promise he'd kept at first. He'd tried. Wanted to believe that they wanted time with him. Wanted to make up for never being there in his childhood, for using him as a weapon against each other in their nasty divorce proceedings. All the signs were there, screaming in his face. The red flags that they were never going to care for him the way other parents cared for their children. And he'd ignored them, until they'd made it impossible to look away.

"I didn't take anything from my parents. I am nothing like them." He hadn't meant to speak the words out loud, but there was no rewinding the tape.

Wren looked away from the tank, her dark gaze holding him in place. "Then what you got from them was choosing to act nothing like them."

His parents were a thing he'd locked away. A piece of his past that got no place in his future.

The last day he'd spoken to his father and mother, they'd all blown up at the other. His father had called him a loser, a piece of crap son. His mother, siding with his father for the first time in at least a decade, had agreed. In that moment, Luca matched his parents' outsize emotions. Screaming all his hurt, his worries… It hadn't made him feel as good as he thought it would.

They still reached out sometimes, text messages, the odd birthday card, always delivered at least a month late. Luca never answered.

"And you?" Luca pushed away the memories, the hurt that still rose too close to the surface if he thought about it too long. "Are you a doctor because of your parents?"

"Yes. But not the right kind of doctor. Plastics was not the specialty they wanted for me. I racked up quite a bit of debt when they cut me off over my choice."

Debt. The word chilled his bones. Every friend who'd ever asked for money started with a soft pitch. A quick word about their debt, their misfortune. Laying the groundwork. But Wren was discussing her parents cutting her off because she'd dared to carve her own path. It was wicked. "They cut you off?"

"Yeah, they wanted me in neurology." She held up her finger, clearly mimicking a parent. "We did not put all this work into you for you to do something other than neurology."

"It's your life." Why did she seem so nonchalant about it?

"Sure." There was no anger in her voice. "I did

my rotation in plastics, and there was no other specialty that held as much interest."

How far does she bury the hurt? It had to be there. Even sunny Wren couldn't just accept this, could she?

He'd heard people talk about finding their specialty as a magic moment. The realization that they were in the exact right space. Sure, there were physicians that went into specific specialties for the money attached to them, but those individuals were few and far between.

Wren was describing the defining moment of her career without any passion. Plastics was one of the hardest specialties to get into. Everything about her was impressive. But if it wasn't what she wanted...

"You wanted marine biology."

Wren let out a little puff of air. "I loved the thought of it, but as you pointed out, I was sixteen when I was ready for grad school. Most of my life was lived in the library getting ready for the next test or quiz. Reading knowledge, absorbing it, but not really living it. That section just interested me more than others when I was twelve. Though Ronan also loved fish. He had a tank in his room, if you remember. So it was a bonding thing. Who knows? Maybe it was just because Ronan loved them. I was basically a kid. Not exactly ready for permanent life decisions."

Luca swallowed the angry words that he couldn't say to her parents. The words had no place to land. She'd been a kid. And they'd pressured her then, cut her off for making the "wrong" choice. And here she was nonchalantly discussing it.

Lifting her hand to his lips, he pressed a kiss to her palm. "I have seen more than one coffee mug that says something like a reader lives a thousand lives." At least she had books.

Wren rolled her eyes and turned back to the tank. "Yeah, I am pretty sure that's attributed to a fantasy author. Did you know that male sea horses are the ones who carry the eggs until they hatch? The female lays the eggs in his brood pouch—think of it as kinda like an underwater kangaroo pouch." She watched another swim by, then looked over her shoulder at him.

"There are thirty-six species of sea horses."

Wren's eyes lit up. "Oh. You know about them, too."

He pressed his lips to her cheek. "I have been here a lot." He pointed to the sign in front of the tank. "Not as impressive as it seems."

"Yes." Wren laid her head on his shoulder. "It is. But you are here for the octopuses, if I recall."

That was his original thought, the animal he most wanted to show off. But now he had a different idea. "We can come back for that another time. What if we do the behind-the-scenes tour for sea horses? They have a world-renowned breeding program."

"Baby sea horses. We can see baby sea horses?" Her eyes were bright, and he was pretty sure she was trying not to do a happy dance. He could give

Wren this experience…and so many others she'd missed out on.

"We absolutely can."

CHAPTER ELEVEN

LUCA PURSED HIS lips waiting for Lena to at least try the new exercise he'd given her. The woman had made so much progress. Her hand was functioning better than he'd thought it would at this stage. That didn't mean it would ever be exactly like it was.

"I shouldn't have come today." Lena brushed a tear away and then let the others just fall.

"Lena—"

"I know, Dr. McDonnell, I have to practice. I have to do the exercises. I have to work at it. But why bother?" She looked at the door, and he wondered if she was about to call their session off.

Lena was an adult. He couldn't order her to stay.

Therese walked in, and Wren followed behind her. The two women had formed a fast friendship. Luca had caught himself wondering over the last week about how much he was going to have to share Wren when Therese and Seth moved into the apartment complex.

A selfish thought indeed. But he enjoyed who he was around Wren. The man she brought out in him.

"Lena!" Wren grinned, walked over and bent down so she was eye level with Lena.

Therese gave him a short nod. So Wren being

here at the same time as Lena wasn't a coincidence. He mouthed *thank you* over Lena and Wren's heads.

"Dr. Freson." Lena tried a smile, but it was clearly faked. "If you're coming to check up on me, I am failing."

"Why?" Wren's gaze was soft, but there was a firmness in her tone. A deliberate one-word question.

"My art is messed up." Lena ran a hand along the skin graft that Wren had overseen. "No matter what I do, it's wrong."

Luca looked at her fingers. They didn't have all their strength back. That would take time, but they were significantly more functional than they were before. She should be able to hold a paintbrush and maneuver it however she wanted. At least for a while. Stamina would come with time.

"How?" Wren still hadn't broken eye contact with Lena.

"It's dark." Lena shook her head. "Everyone always chatted up the brightness. I'm an expert on light. And now it's vanished."

Luca could not pretend to know what that meant. "Shadows are light."

Lena rolled her eyes. "Shadows are areas without light."

"Shadows answer to light. They are the absence." Wren pulled a pencil from her coat pocket. "How well are you holding things like this?"

Her dark gaze floated to him, and he nodded. Lena's hands were tight. Because she hadn't done the exercises at home he'd recommended? This would let him see exactly how she was handling it, without it coming directly from the physical therapist.

Lena moved the pencil through her fingers, grimacing as she clutched it. But she didn't let go. Didn't drop or throw it. Progress. "It's uncomfortable. But I can hold it like this for an hour before the pain is too much."

"An hour?" Luca snapped his mouth shut. The issue wasn't underuse. Lena was pushing herself. Hurting herself. Because she needed to feel like herself. A person she no longer knew.

"Yes. An hour. I used to stand in my studio with my hands moving for hours! And my hands cramped then but not like this. Not making it impossible. And the colors won't come." Now she was gripping the pencil like she was going to throw the offending object.

"Lena, take a deep breath." Luca's words were firm. Throwing the pencil might feel good for a moment. But she'd feel guilty later. And that guilt would slow her down.

Lena followed the order and then passed the pencil back to Wren.

"Reinventing yourself isn't easy," Wren said. "I know."

Was Wren reinventing herself? *Yes.* That was part of the reason she was in San Diego.

Lena looked skeptical. "You ever reinvented yourself after your world was destroyed?"

"Yes." Wren took a deep breath. "My brother was

killed in a car accident. I lost the person I could lean on. The one who would always answer the phone." She hesitated for a moment. Weighing her next words? Her gaze darted to Luca. Words she didn't want him hearing?

"I had planned to be a marine biologist. I was enrolled in a masters program for it."

Whoa. That was more information than she'd given him before. It wasn't a path she'd looked at. It was a path she planned to follow.

"My brother was my biggest cheerleader and a barrier between my parents who had other ideas. When I lost him, I lost the ability to fight. For years. Ended up in med school, and I would have ended up a neurologist if my parents had their way. I fought back before residency. It cost me."

The sea horses. It was more than just a passing fancy, but she hadn't shared that with him. He wasn't sure why that stung so much. But he knew the cost. The debt. The thing her parents intentionally burdened her with.

"Now I'm a plastic surgeon specializing in burn care. I make the difference I want. However, it is a different dream."

"Do you miss that first dream?"

"Sometimes." Wren tilted her head, then pointed to the skin graft. "But it passes quickly. You are still the woman that painted light into every corner. She will always be a part of you. Now she has expanded."

"I didn't want to expand." Lena looked at the

pencil Wren had left on the small table she was working on.

"I know. I didn't, either."

Luca had to swallow to make his tongue function. There were so many statements in this short conversation. Insights to help Lena but revelations about the woman he'd woken beside this morning, too. Revelations she hadn't shared with him. Even when he was with her behind the scenes at the aquarium.

"The next steps will be hard, but there is beauty and growth that comes with the hard steps." Wren's voice wobbled just a little but Luca doubted Lena noticed. Then Wren looked at him and grinned.

How was the woman able to smile after just admitting that her life wasn't her choice? That what she'd wanted wasn't considered?

It was one thing to not buy a stuffed toy or celebrate her birthday. Her parents had changed the course of her life. Forced her into a career path. Then gotten angry when she'd finally charted her own course.

"And I bet those paintings you are so angry at are gorgeous." Luca kept his gaze firmly rooted on Lena as he offered the advice. If he looked at Wren, he was terrified a wave of words would flood out. Demands. Worries. Hurt.

"Do you have any pictures of them?" Therese asked.

Lena had mentioned, when she was focused on her therapy a few weeks ago, that she took photos of every canvas at all the stages. Just so she could see the painting come to life. He was willing to bet her phone had at least one image of the creations she claimed to hate.

Lena shrugged and pulled her phone out. It was an angry sea. Dark waters competing with a dark sky, the moon barely adding its graceful light to the dance.

"It's breathtaking." Therese's voice was quiet, her hand over her heart. "What's it called?"

He was glad Therese was able to comment because the image had stolen all thoughts from him. It was captivating. If this was what Lena considered failure, then what was her definition of success?

"It doesn't have one. Not yet. My agent keeps trying to get me to name it. Wants it up on my website. Says it will bring in at least a quarter of a million dollars."

If it went for auction, Luca suspected it would fetch quite a bit more. Hell, he'd reach out to the agent and see what the price was. He could put it in his living room. The evening sun hitting the shadows… It would be perfect.

"Shadow storms." Wren's hand flew to her lips. "Sorry, as we can tell, I'm not great at creative things."

Lena's head shifted as she tilted the picture back and forth, her gaze rooted to the screen. "No. That actually makes sense. I might steal it."

Wren beamed. "It's yours if you want it." She looked at her watch. "I need to get to rounds, but as I know Dr. McDonnell is going to tell you, you're pushing yourself too much. Your hand needs time to recover. You shouldn't have any pain." She started to stand, then took one more look at the image. "This is a masterpiece. Maybe it doesn't feel that way right now. Doesn't make it untrue. Let me know which museum purchases it. I want to know where to visit it in all its glory." Wren offered Lena one more smile and then a quick one for him, and she was off.

"Dr. Freson is right."

"About this being a masterpiece?" Lena was still focused on the painting. So much of physical therapy wasn't about the exercises but the life the person wanted, needed to live. Lena had hit a plateau. Not because of therapy but because of life outside of therapy.

"Yes. But also about you needing to not overdo it." He held up a hand, forestalling the fight he could see building in Lena's eyes. Good. Fighting was good. He could work with fighting. "Next week, I want you to bring your largest and smallest brushes." He held up the stress ball they'd been using for weeks. "I think it's time we transitioned to a new tool."

Wren blinked and tried to fully relax her shoulders but her body was tighter than ever. Why on earth had she let so many things out with Lena?

Yes, the woman was struggling. And yes, Wren understood the feeling of losing yourself. It was easier to comply when Ronan was gone than to fight. And she loved the work she did. That didn't mean there weren't times, like behind the scenes at the aquarium, that she didn't wonder what might have been if her parents had seen past the genius and just loved her.

But everyone had what-ifs in life.

If she hadn't chosen this field, the Link-Freson technique might not exist. That procedure changed lives. It made a difference. This was why she didn't look back at the possibilities. Why she buried it in sunshine.

"Dr. Freson!" The nurse running toward her was pale.

Wren didn't know what had happened, but today's plans had just shifted exponentially. She ran to the nurse, who turned and started back toward the ER. Wren matched her pace. "Details." The more she had now, the quicker she could react.

"Kitchen worker. Twenty-three. Pressure cooker was making weird noises, and they leaned over just as the lid popped off. Steam burn. Full face. You're needed in the ER."

Her stomach sank. Pressure cookers were excellent and saved time. But when they malfunctioned, the devastation could be extensive.

"Why didn't you page me?"

"System down. Guess those budget cuts from last year are coming home to roost." The nurse pushed open the door of the ER, and the screams coming from the bed down the hall were clear.

"Why the hell isn't he sedated?" Or at least under extensive pain meds. Though the fact that he still had feeling was in some ways a good thing. It meant the nerves were intact.

"The pain meds were pushed. But…"

But they weren't working.

Wren walked into the room, the horror show clear around her. The man was burned from the face down across his chest. There were also cuts, and he'd need extensive reconstruction.

Dr. Michaels, a trauma surgeon, didn't turn as he barked out orders to get the man under and get a surgical suite ready.

Wren washed her hands, gloved up and moved over to take a look. The burns were extensive. The skin was already pulling away.

A person Wren didn't recognize stepped to the door, and Scott, an ER nurse, stepped away from the bed. "I do not care if you need a report. I do not care if you want to cover your ass."

"Scott!" One of the other nurses was already trying to get the angry nurse under control.

"Get your company ready, because they will answer—"

"Scott!" Wren's shout seemed to catch the nurse off guard. "Now is not the time."

"They want him to check some box and sign away his worker's compensation." Scott stepped into the hall, and less than a second later, security was carting away whoever had decided it was a good idea to reach their employee when they were in a literal medical crisis.

"All right, everyone!" Dr. Michaels called over the chaos. "We are heading to surgical. Now!"

Wren stretched her arm over her head as she waited for the water to boil. She'd planned a more extensive dinner than buttered noodles and garlic bread, but surgery had taken it out of her.

That did not mean she wasn't looking forward to dinner with Luca and snuggling Hippo. He still didn't let the poor guy up on his couch, but in *this* apartment the dog was her snuggle companion. Though Luca was right when he pointed out that Wren snuggled Luca, and Hippo flopped on the other side of the couch, more hanging on than snuggling. She still thought it counted.

A knock came at the door, and Wren called for the two of them to enter.

"Hi, honey." Luca walked in, kissed her cheek, then pulled out a giant bouquet of flowers. Reds, yellows and a smattering of blue.

"Oh my gosh." She couldn't take her eyes off them. "This is so sweet." Wren started to reach for them and then paused, her hands hanging in thin air as she spun around her kitchen. What was she supposed to put them in?

A vase. Duh.

An easy answer. Assuming one had a vase. "I don't think I have a vase." She turned back to look at the bunch of stems... Perhaps a really large cup?

"Don't think? You aren't sure whether you have a vase? Are these your first flowers?" Scarlet invaded Luca's cheeks as soon as the question was out. "They are, aren't they?"

Wren shrugged. She'd had a lot of experiences in her life as a child prodigy, but that cocoon didn't let in a whole host of experiences most people got in their teen and early twenties.

"You're my first boyfriend, so it makes some sense that these are my first flowers." *Boyfriend.* The title was out, hanging in the open. They'd technically never addressed their status. They were together nearly every night. They planned days off together. Drove to the hospital together when they were on the same shifts. A little over a month of being nearly inseparable.

But the words boyfriend and girlfriend were left completely out of the discussion. It had simply rolled off her tongue. A poetic declaration just waiting for confirmation.

"I know I'm your first." Was there a tiny edge on the word *first*?

Wren reached for the flowers to give her hands something to do. She'd had a long day. Looking for pinpoint signs was how she'd lived with her parents. An attempt to stay ahead of their ever-shifting moods. She hadn't lived that way in years, and there was no reason to start now.

"But flowers, Wren? You've graduated college—"

"At sixteen." She gave him a wink, hoping to loosen whatever had tensed his shoulders.

The quip clearly didn't help. "And med school at

nineteen. People bring flowers to both those events. Your family didn't even bother?"

What was there to say? She'd asked for a toy when she was eleven. Begged for it. It was the first thing she remember truly craving. And they'd told her no. Expecting something like flowers for achieving what they expected of her was hardly something she'd consider.

"I like that there aren't roses. The hibiscus reds with the dark center are fantastic. And the lilies! I have never seen a yellow so deep. But I don't know what these are." Her finger touched the tiny blue flowers.

"You know hibiscus and lilies but not forget-me-nots?" Luca's smile eased the tension away from his eyes—almost all the way.

"I guess so." She started looking through her cabinet as the timer over the oven went off. "Grab the noodles and toss them in the drainer please." Why were all of her cups regular size? "Hope you don't mind buttered noodles. After the surgery, I didn't have time to make the planned meal." Maybe she could put the flowers in a giant bowl?

Luca turned the timer off, dumped the water from the pot and then wrapped his arms around her waist. "I don't mind at all—also, I have a vase upstairs. I'll grab it while you put the finishing touches on this."

Wren leaned her head against his shoulder and pressed her lips to his. "My hero."

"Uh-huh." He gave her derrière a quick tap, then headed out the door.

Wren waited for a moment, then looked at Hippo. "Do you think he didn't register that I called him my boyfriend or was he ignoring it?"

The giant head tilted one way and then the other. "Not a lot of help, buddy. At least you're cute."

CHAPTER TWELVE

HE WAS THE first to bring her flowers. That thought had kept him up far too long last night. Wren lay in his arms, her nude body snuggled so close. His hand traced up her hip, so slowly, careful not to wake the beauty next to him.

There were far better thoughts he could pass the time with, but it was that one that kept running through his mind.

First boyfriend, too.

Luca had known that. But somehow hearing it from her sweet lips last night brought that truth to the forefront of his mind.

Firsts were important. Milestones. Wren had had so few experiences. She deserved the world. And any choice she wanted.

His heart clenched as the sun started pouring through her window. They slept at his place most nights. He wasn't sure why she'd asked to stay here.

Keeping some of herself apart?

He didn't think that was what was happening. But if it was, that was her right.

He was falling for her. Who was he trying to convince when there was no one with him but his thoughts? He'd fallen for her. Hard.

Love.

Luca's gaze roamed her face. Even in sleep, there was a soft lift to the ends of her lips. Wren smiled even when she was asleep. His little ray of sunshine. He loved her.

And if she fell for him, it would be another first. His heartbeat pounded in his ears. Wren loving him. Holding him. He craved it.

But she deserved everything. Her parents stole her childhood, and then the career she wanted. The universe, in its cruelty, stole Ronan. She'd never dated before Luca. Never lain with another.

First loves were sweet. But there was a reason people called them *first* loves. More tended to follow.

Luca pressed his lips to her head. He would love Wren for however long she wanted. And if she decided she wanted more adventures, he'd find a way to step aside.

Wren let out a little sigh and rolled over. Her sunshine blasting his soul.

"You look like rough thoughts are traveling through your mind?" Her fingers pressed lightly against his temples. "Should I kiss the thoughts away?"

He dropped a kiss on her nose. "I won't say no to kisses, but this is just my face before I've had coffee."

Wren raised an eyebrow, but she didn't call out the lie. Her hand slipped down his thigh, her fingernails grazing his skin. His manhood rose to the occasion instantly.

"I like being able to turn you on so easily." Her dark gaze held his as she cupped him.

"Wren—"

"Mm-hmm, when you say my name like that."

He reached his hand up to skim her nipples, but she pulled away.

"You said you needed coffee, but I think there's another way to force whatever you don't want to tell me out of your brain." Her lips traveled down his body, kissing him nearly up to his manhood, then easing away.

"Tease!" His hands ran over her head, the only part he could touch in this moment. When her tongue swept his shaft, he let out a groan. Her mouth captured him. Luca resisted the primal urge to buck as her tongue swirled the tip of his erection.

He craved this. Craved her, but it wasn't enough. "Wren." Placing his hand beneath her chin, Luca pressed up until she was looking at him. He grabbed a condom from the side table and couldn't contain his smile as she ripped the package open.

Wren's hands wrapped around his length as she leisurely unrolled the condom down his length.

"Tease."

She threw a leg over him and pressed her opening to the tip of him but no farther. "You've already called me a tease. Now I feel honor bound to make sure I've earned the title." Wren lowered herself just a hair.

His finger ran along her nipple, twirling until it

was perky and hard. She wasn't the only one who knew exactly how to drive the other mad.

Gripping his free hand, she guided it to her center. Forcing it exactly where she needed it. Damn. This woman would be his undoing.

Luca knew the exact pressure, the exact movements to bring her to oblivion. Part of him ached to rush through them. Make sure she was panting as she fully took him.

But this was her morning. She was in charge. Demanding what she wanted.

It was the hottest thing ever.

She squeezed him with her core and glided down him. Her head fell back as he filled her completely.

"Lean back." Luca let the words out between his teeth. He needed to come, but that was not happening until Wren tripped over the edge.

She didn't ask questions, didn't resist. She simply laid her hands on thighs and leaned back. She was fully open to him now. His thumb stroked her as she moved against him.

As soon as he felt her clinch, he sat up a little, pulled her to him and drove himself into her until he'd claimed her completely.

Wren slid off him but didn't move from his chest. "That has to be the best way to start a morning."

If there was something better, he had no interest in searching it out.

"You got your place packed up?" Wren sipped her coffee as she added in her notes regarding a patient she'd seen in the ER. The actress had demanded a plastic surgeon to make sure she had as little scarring as possible.

The ER doc had been less than impressed with Wren when she commented that it shouldn't only be people in the public sphere who got the option. Most people didn't realize that plastics was able to stitch up any skin, not just surgeries, to ensure the best scar outcome. It should be offered to everyone, particularly if the scar was on the face.

"Nearly." Seth tapped in his notes. "I hate putting these in."

"Certainly not what we went to med school for." Wren laughed. "I've joked with Luca that maybe we should find a way to hire assistants to do our charting for us. He was fully onboard."

"He could afford that." Seth continued typing away. "Wonder if he's ever floated it by HR? They won't provide the service, but if he contracted out, they'd probably let it slide."

"I mean, I doubt he could actually afford it. But it is a nice dream." Wren wasn't sure why the joke she'd made suddenly felt like it was far more serious.

Seth looked up from his terminal. "Wren, he owns the building. I am sure from the rent alone he could hire three assistants. In fact, if he decides that, tell him I claim the third."

She laughed. "Oh no. He owns his apartment. It's the entire top floor." The words poured out, and the truth started to register. No. He couldn't. "Owning your penthouse suite is wildly impressive. But he doesn't own the building."

Seth pursed his lips, with a look she worried was pity carried in his bright gaze.

"No. He'd have told me." Even as she said the words, Wren wasn't sure they were the full truth. "Are you sure?"

"Yeah. I was curious about the place after the rental agent got weird with us. I mean, she acted like we were trying to pull a fast one on the rent." Seth shrugged. "It made sense once I realized. I mean, claiming to know the owner of the building is what a scam artist would do. Though I will admit I was tempted to ask if he could use his ownership connections to let us move in tomorrow so we have a full three days to get settled before shifts start again."

Seth's chuckle wasn't full. The joke was a half-hearted attempt to rectify an uncomfortable situation.

Her notes were done. She needed to leave. Take a few minutes to gather her thoughts.

"Why didn't he tell me?" The question was out before she knew it. "Sorry, inside head thought."

"Understood. I, um, actually wanted to ask you if you and McSteamy might want to help us move in this weekend. Therese swears she can lift the boxes, but with the baby and all, but I um—"

"It's fine, Seth. I am sure that we can be there. Just have Therese text me the details." She headed out. She needed a moment, more than a moment to work through all the tumbling thoughts in her head.

They'd lain in bed this morning, every morning over the last month. They'd gone to the aquarium and had so many movie nights.

But when I mentioned the situation with Therese, he seemed short.

"Hi there, sunshine." Luca popped beside her, a cup of coffee in his hands. "You look pensive."

"Do you own our building?" The question was out, and she crossed her arms. "No. Don't answer that. This isn't the place for this discussion. Actually, maybe it is. Do you?"

There were too many thoughts racing through her mind. He owned the building. And hadn't told her.

"Does it matter?"

"My boyfriend can buy whatever he wants, including buildings, and doesn't tell me. Yes, it matters." Wren crossed her arms. How could it not matter?

"Why? You looking for a huge payout?" The playful look in his eyes vanished. His chin raised slightly. This was McSteamy standing before her. Not Luca.

So, the answer was yes, he owned the building. And he didn't want her knowing. That stung.

"Because." Not a great answer, but she wasn't sure why it bothered her so much that he'd kept it from her. It felt purposeful. And there had seemed like times when he was holding back.

He said an investment hit big. There was an investment hitting big, and there was owning prime real estate in the most expensive city in the whole country.

"Why does it actually matter, Wren?"

Wren looked at her feet, tears threatening to push their way out. "Why not tell me? Why are you hiding it?"

"I wasn't."

When she met his gaze, she saw him flinch. "Come on, Luca." She couldn't do this. Not here. Not now. She wanted, needed, more information. But in a place where they could actually discuss it.

"I need to see a patient." Wren stepped around him, her body tight as she tried to figure out why he wouldn't want her to know. It didn't matter.

Maybe it does?

Turning the corner, she waited a minute. Hoping that he might chase her down. Might come clean. Might say something that didn't mean she'd asked a question and opened a gulf between them.

The gulf was always there. He just didn't want me to know.

Wren got to the door of the patient's room and mentally shook herself. She was here to check in on Cristan Bell, the man who'd taken a steam bath straight to the face. He was wrapped in gauze and medicated to make him as comfortable as possible.

"Good morning, Cristan," Wren said, entering the room. There was a woman sitting on the couch, a big pillow next to her. "I'm Dr. Freson, the plastic surgeon."

"Nadia, Cristan's wife."

The man turned toward their voices, "Is it morning?" His eyes were bandaged tightly. The burns over his eyelids were horrific. He'd need at least half a dozen facial reconstruction surgeries, if not more.

"It is. A bright sunny morning."

Cristan's head tilted a little. "Not sure San Diego knows how to create any other weather."

Wren nodded, then caught herself. Cristan couldn't pick up on nonverbal cues right now. "It is certainly nice. I lived on the east coast before heading here. I don't miss the winter and chilly rain."

"You will." Cristan turned his head toward the window, though he couldn't see the sun. "Or maybe not, Nadia has never missed the snow."

Nadia pushed a tear away from her cheek. "We used to live in northern Ohio. Lake effect snow, meant we got three to four feet of the white stuff at a time. I like the sun, but I do miss the seasons." Her gaze traveled over her husband as more silent tears fell.

"How are you feeling today?" Wren looked at the chart. The man never requested pain meds. Never complained. He was the perfect patient according to the nursing staff.

That did not align with his injuries.

"Fine."

She was certain that was a lie. "How are you actually feeling?"

"Fine." There was no emotion in the word. No hint that he was anything other than fine. She wanted to believe him. Maybe she would if the night nurse hadn't noted that his fingers tapped when he was in pain—at least she thought they did.

Right now, the fingers of his right hand were bouncing off his thigh in a rhythmic fashion. If the nurse was right, and Wren saw no reason to doubt her, then Cristan was hiding a decent amount of discomfort.

"I am going to get a drink. Do you want me to bring you back a smoothie?" Nadia laid a hand against his knee.

"Mango, if they have it."

"You know they only have banana and strawberry." Nadia kissed the top of his head, the only place on his face not covered with white gauze.

"I know. But if you keep asking, they might realize what a mistake they've made in not having the best flavor."

"Not sure that's how it works, but I will be back in a little while." Nadia looked back at Wren as she reached for the door and mouthed a sentence. *Ask him how he feels when I'm gone.* Then she went out the door and pulled it closed, firmly enough to make sure that it was clear she had left.

"Do you want to tell me how you feel now?" Wren moved toward Cristan. She needed to get a look at the wounds and see if they were on track to schedule his next surgery.

"I'm sore. But handling it." Cristan let out a sigh. "Nadia is worried I'll hold this against her."

Wren started gently pulling back on the gauze.

"Was she at the plant kitchen when the accident happened?"

"No." Cristan flinched but didn't let out a noise as a piece of gauze caught on his cheek. Wren used a bit of gel to wet the gauze down, then started to pull it back slowly. "We moved here for her job. She's the main manager at the biggest hotel in the city. A real big promotion from the place she managed in Cleveland." The pride in his voice was palpable.

"But my job didn't transfer. I've worked odd jobs here and there. The plant kitchen doesn't pay well, and it's dangerous. Obviously." He gestured to his face. "She thinks that it's her fault. If she'd turned down the job offer, then we'd still be in Cleveland." He shrugged as the final piece of gauze came away. "She deserved the promotion. And this is the company's fault."

His burns had to hurt. His face must ache.

"You're hiding the pain to make sure she doesn't feel worse." Wren made a note in the chart. They needed to make sure that Nadia was out of the room to get the proper answer. Protecting each other was sweet, but it might hurt Cristan's recovery in the long run. "I know you don't want her to know. But she knows. Maybe not all of it but enough. Let her in. Let her help you through all of this, Cristan."

The man nodded, but Wren wasn't sure he planned to follow through with any of it.

Would Luca ever let her in? She didn't know… and that terrified her.

CHAPTER THIRTEEN

W𝚛ᴇɴ ᴇxɪᴛᴇᴅ ᴛʜᴇ elevator but hesitated as she started toward Luca's door. The plan was to come here. At least it had been before she confronted him at the hospital. Not her smoothest moment.

It was just so shocking. He owned the building.

She waited another minute, then purposefully made herself move forward. They needed to discuss this. She had to understand why he hadn't told her.

Her knuckles rapped on the door, and Hippo's excited bark echoed into the hallway. Luca opened the door, but he didn't step back to let her in. The distant look in his eyes made her throat seize.

She waited a moment, hoping he'd laugh or step back or say something! Anything.

Instead it was her putting out the first words. "Are you going to let me in, or do I stand out here to have the conversation?"

"If you are here to talk about the building, then there is nothing to discuss." Luca shrugged.

"Like hell there isn't." Wren crossed her arms over herself to keep from pushing past him. This was his home. She wouldn't invade it. At least with him owning the floor, it meant there were no nosy neighbors seeking reasons to walk down the hall for a better look at the drama.

"Why didn't you tell me?" She'd told him so many things. Opened up and shared secrets no one knew. And he'd never done the same. A fact she'd realized this afternoon.

"Why does it matter?" Luca leaned an arm on the doorway. If they weren't arguing, it'd be sexy.

It was like they were repeating the script from this afternoon. Not getting anywhere. Wren shook her head. When she was growing up, the adults around her, fellow students and colleagues had done the same. Shielding her from bad news. Protecting her. It all boiled down to the same thing, keeping secrets from her instead of treating her as an equal.

"You told me you owned the apartment. Why not say you owned the building? That is more than an investment hitting big."

"It is." Two words. No inflection to them.

He owed her the truth.

"What is it you want, Wren? Might as well let it out."

"I want the truth, Luca." She waited a second, but he didn't respond. "You don't trust me with the answer." She said the words more to herself. A person wasn't an equal to someone they couldn't trust. The walls of the hallway felt like they were closing in. This wasn't happening. It wasn't.

His mouth opened, but he didn't say anything.

"Okay. Yeah." Filler words. Words her brain spat out while it was still reeling with the information forcing its way through. He didn't trust her. Didn't want her to know. If Seth hadn't let the information out...

Her chest ached, and blood rushed to her face. Without trust what was this?

Nothing. Such a simple, painful word.

"Fine, Luca. You don't need to tell me. If you'll just pack my clothes up and send them to my place." She had months left on her rental agreement. And then there were the hospital run-ins—at least that was something she could avoid.

Mostly.

A tear slipped down her cheek, and she headed for the stairwell. There was no way she was waiting for the elevator when they were the only people on the floor.

"You want your stuff?"

The words hit her back, but she didn't have the strength to turn around. "Yes, please."

"Wait, you really want your stuff? *That* is what you want? All you want?"

Was this some kind of joke? Whatever it was, her heart was too broken to play along. "Luca, I am tired, and honestly broken by this."

That was probably too honest, but she didn't have it in her to cover the truth. She'd fallen for him. Hard. And yet, she didn't know him. Not this part of him, the McSteamy persona he wore so well for others. He was different with her. That was true. She'd thought that meant more than it did apparently.

"Yes, I want my stuff. I will keep my distance at the hospital until we're more comfortable." Who was she kidding? She wasn't going to be comfortable around him. Ever.

Wren hit the stairwell, grateful to get away. She was halfway down the stairwell when she heard her name. Her feet paused, despite her brain ordering them to run on.

"What!" She rounded on him, tears streaking down her face. What could he possibly want?

"You don't want anything?" He reached for her, but she stepped back.

"I told you, I want my stuff. You don't trust me. You don't want me knowing your secrets. Fine. I shared so much with you, and you've shared nothing. I get it." She didn't get it. Not really, but she was not going to puzzle it out here. With him.

The tears were truly streaming now. But now most of them were from anger. How dare he draw this out?

"I meant, you don't want me to pay for your apartment? Or go on some fancy trip? Pay off your student loan. Or—"

"No, Luca. I don't want anything from you other than the stuff I left at your place. I don't know what sick game you're playing, but I am done with it."

"Wren." He started for her again, and this time she took two steps down. "I'm confused."

He was confused? He was the one who started all of this. The one who hadn't trusted. The one keeping secrets. "Then let me make it really clear. Whatever this was, is over. You don't trust me, and I shared all my secrets with you. Told you—" She'd confessed that she'd wanted another job. That she'd never gotten a birthday present. Her desire for a kid's stuffed toy. That she felt alone and othered. Personal stuff. Deep. Hard.

Instead of sharing with her, he'd hidden something. That might have been okay, if he wasn't so defensive when she found out. It was so clear that he didn't want her knowing.

"I thought you'd want something. Want me to buy something for you."

Wren let out a shrill laugh. "Sure. I find out my boyfriend owns a building, so he must be my bank now. Wow. I really did make a bad impression." They'd spent nearly every night together, and he could jump to such a stupid conclusion.

"Everyone else does." Luca pushed his hands through his hair and sighed.

Those were tragic words hinting at betrayal that unfortunately she knew nothing about. Because he'd shared none of it with her. And, even if that were the case, she'd never given him any reason to expect she'd follow that same path.

"I wouldn't have thought I'd be lumped into 'everyone else.'" She used her fingers for air quotes. "Which is also absolutely false because Seth and Therese know. And have known for at least a week. And unless I am mistaken, the only help they've requested is with moving in."

His eyes widened. Maybe with understanding, but probably because she hadn't told him yet that they'd asked for help with the move.

"Or is it just the women you sleep with who you think look at you like a cash withdrawal machine?" The words turned her stomach. To be reduced to such a level.

"Wren—"

"Everything okay up there, Dr. McDonnell?" The security guard's words floated up the stairwell, cutting off whatever Luca planned to say.

"Fine," Luca called down.

She shook her head. Wren had no words left. She was empty. So she turned on her heel and fled before he could say anything else.

Not that he'd said much anyway.

Luca stood in the stairwell not sure how he'd screwed up so badly. No, that wasn't true. He knew exactly how.

He'd seen Wren's look in the hallway at the hospital. Heard the words, *my boyfriend can buy whatever he wants*, and decided the moment he'd feared was upon him. Rather than acknowledge the fact that he hadn't told her, his walls had slammed down. He'd accused her of wanting something.

And instead of apologizing for it tonight, he'd waited for the hammer that always fell to drop. He was prepped to hear it. Shield at the ready and heart closed off.

Those words never materialized, though.

Her accusations were fair. She'd accused him of not trusting her. Of not telling her anything. Not sharing.

The worst part was she wasn't wrong. He'd listened to her hidden truths. Kissed the tears off her cheeks. Each time she'd asked anything about his past, about anything deeper than his day-to-day activities, he'd pulled back. Retreated.

He'd worried that when she found out, he'd lose her.

I did.

But this time it was because he'd trashed everything. Wren had wanted his truths, not his wallet. Rather than accept that incredible gift, he'd tossed it away. Thrown it away.

His feet were moving. Heading to her floor. There might not be a way to repair this, but she was owed the answers he'd kept from her.

Stepping onto her floor, his feet were suddenly boulders. It felt like hours passed as he walked to her door. She might not answer.

He deserved that.

Standing before her door, he wished he had something to apologize with. Then he shook his head. He'd brought cupcakes before; this time he brought truths.

He raised his fist and wasn't surprised to hear her yell to go away.

"Wren, please. I need to say something. Then I'll go if you want." He raised his voice to make sure she heard him. He wasn't surprised when one of the neighbors opened her door and peeked out.

One nice thing about having it out on his floor was that no one had been there to watch.

Wren's door opened, just a crack. She didn't open it any wider. He waited a moment, then stepped in.

She was already back in the kitchen. The bottle of wine she'd said she was saving was open on the counter.

He didn't know what she was saving it for, but he was certain it wasn't a massive fight with her boyfriend.

She lifted the glass to her lips and stared at him.

"You opened the wine?" It wasn't what he meant to say. Not what was important.

"Yeah, well, I am nowhere near paying off my student loans, so I figure I can get another when that day finally comes." She took a deep sip. "And no, that is *not* a request for you to pay anything off."

He deserved that. Luca waited a minute, then pushed his hands into his pockets. "I am worth over six hundred million dollars."

Wren took another sip of her drink. As if the bombshell he'd held so tight meant nothing.

"I haven't met with my investment advisor this quarter, so it is probably safe to say it's a decent amount more given the state of the real estate market. This isn't the only rental complex I own."

She let out a huff. "I don't care how much you're worth. If that's what you came to tell me, you can leave."

She didn't care. Words he'd longed to hear. Words she meant. He was a damn fool.

"I told Madeline about inheriting Maude's estate two months before we were supposed to wed. The estate was large, and the investments have made it larger over the last ten years."

Wren drained the last of her glass and poured another healthy amount. "I cannot emphasize enough how much I do not care about your investments and the amount they are worth."

"I know."

"Do you?" She raised her glass and tilted her head. The sunshine soul was a storm cloud.

He'd done that. Stolen the beams.

He sucked in a breath. "I walked into the bridal suite on our wedding day and heard her telling her maid of honor about the inheritance. They were laughing because she'd planned to end the engagement the night I told her about the money. She was seeing someone on the side, but she cut it off as soon as she knew she was marrying into a sum greater than she had ever imagined."

Wren sipped her drink but didn't say anything.

Luca took a deep breath. "She was joking that she could spend a few years with me to get half, since I didn't ask for a prenup. Maybe even have a kid or two, so she'd get child support."

Wren's eyes widened. "That is evil."

"Yeah." Evil was a solid word for it. He'd been an unwanted kid. To joke about doing the same for child support... He couldn't even imagine.

"After I ended things, she made sure pretty much everyone in our hometown knew, even though I'd asked her not to say anything." He scoffed. "A final revenge. My friends suddenly saw me differently.

All except Ronan. He only ever asked me to co-sign a loan."

"It doesn't surprise me that he didn't change." Wren shifted. "So your big secret is that you're worth more money than anyone else I know, and you thought I would hear that and demand a healthy slice." She shook her head. "I made quite the negative impression then."

"Wren." He took a step toward her. "You didn't. This was my fault. All my fault. Everyone always changes when they know."

"Everyone but Ronan. And Seth. And Therese. And me." She let out a breath. "Actually, that isn't true. I have changed. I am furious and heartbroken. Most people see me as a genius. A prodigy. Naive little Wren. You're the first to see me as a gold digger."

He deserved that.

"Is there any way for me to make this up?" He'd grovel. Do anything. But if she wanted him to leave, he'd do it. Accept the fact that he'd destroyed the thing that brought him peace. The woman who made him feel whole.

"What if I say pay off my student loan?" Her voice shook.

His eyes shot wide. This was a test, and he needed to pass it. Wren wasn't interested in his money. She'd made that very clear.

"I don't think that is what you really want." He took a step toward her.

Her bottom lip was trembling, but she wasn't telling him to get out. "What do I want, Luca?" She raised her chin, her dark gaze holding him.

He had one chance to bridge the chasm he'd created. What she wanted—needed was the truth.

"The truth."

She raised a brow. "Which is?"

He took another step toward her. Close enough to touch her but not reaching for her. "I panicked today because I love you. And the thought of losing you to what I've lost everyone to sent me into a spiral. It is not fair, and it's not right, but I wanted that distance, so when you came to the door to ask the favor everyone else seemed to want from me, it wouldn't hurt as bad."

"Did that work?" She set down the still mostly full wineglass.

He tilted his head. "I think we both know this is a textbook definition of something very much *not* working. I royally screwed up. In fact, if someone wants to put my picture next the words *screw up* in an online dictionary, I could not blame them."

"Screw up is two words. I don't think it's in the dictionary."

He chuckled. "It's acknowledged slang. I am pretty sure it's in there. But we can look it up? Set that part of the argument aside."

"Luca."

He held his breath. His life revolved around this moment. Whatever she decided, he'd find a way to deal with it.

"I don't—" Her voice caught, and the world around him darkened.

Breathe.

"I don't want your money. I wanted you."

Past tense. Damn it.

She looked at him. "Do you trust me?" She held up a hand before he could say anything, "I mean really trust me? If I make a joke about you paying for something, are you going to see that as me stepping into the role you've assigned everyone else?"

It was the easiest answer he'd ever had. "Completely. I trust you completely, Wren." He was stunned by how true that was.

Stepping up to her, Luca hesitated for only a second before reaching for her. As her hand wrapped through his, he finally felt like he could breathe again. "I love you, Wren. I trust you."

She laid her head against his shoulder, letting out a soft sigh. Wren didn't say anything, but that was okay. She was in his arms. He had another chance. One he did not plan on screwing up again.

CHAPTER FOURTEEN

HE LOVED HER. Wren rolled over, her gaze falling on Luca's still slumbering face. They'd come back to his place last night. Talked more.

He'd opened up about his parents demanding money. Calling him all sorts of names when he reminded them that they'd ignored him until it benefited them. How lost and alone it made him feel. And telling her how Maude said the money was cursed.

Wren bit her lip. He believed that. At least to some extent. He'd opened up—fully. Answered any question she asked. Held her hand and kissed her lips.

And she still hadn't been able to say the words back. She loved him. It was the only reason she'd let him into her place last night, her heart so broken, hoping for a miracle.

One Luca delivered.

So why was the truth still buried deep in her chest?

Because for a moment, he'd seen her as something she'd never been. *Gold digger.*

Not that he'd used that word. But there was no other term. The man who'd never treated her as an outcast or called her a genius had picked something different.

He'd also apologized. Something no one else did.

Apologized, then told her he loved her.

But what if he still didn't really see her?

It was an unfair question.

Is it?

He stirred, and she forced the worry to the back of her head. Today was a new day. Wren was an expert at finding bright spots and marching on. Luca loved her. He loved her.

From this moment on, she was looking forward. Period.

"Wren?" Luca said her name like he was a little surprised to still find her in his bed.

"Expect me to vanish?" She ran her hand down his cheek. The stubble of his beard was rough under her hands.

Luca grabbed her free hand, pulling it to his lips. "Maybe."

She grinned. "Well, I am still here, but I forgot with everything going on yesterday. Seth made a joke, but I think we can probably make good on it anyway. Provided you are willing to use a little of your leverage as owner of the building."

Luca kissed her fingers again. "What joke?"

Not an immediate yes. But not an unqualified no, either. That was progress. "Given that Seth, Therese and both of us are off until Monday—"

"Three-day weekend!" Luca grinned, a full smile. One free of worry.

"Yes, well, they aren't supposed to get the keys to their place until tomorrow, but he joked about asking you to see if he could get them today to give them an extra day." Wren rubbed his cheek. "He doesn't know I'm asking. I think he used it to try to lighten the mood after he let out your secret. But I mean—"

Luca laid a finger against her lips. "I'll make the call now." He reached for his phone, placed the call and made sure they'd reach out to Seth as quickly as possible.

So easy. No hesitation. No worry that someone was taking advantage of him.

As soon as he hung up, her lips were on his.

His hands slipped down her back as he pulled her on top of him. They'd slept in clothes for the first time in weeks last night.

Luca's fingers traced along her back but didn't slide up her shirt.

She laid her forehead against his, breathing in his soft scent. There was no agenda here. No move to make love. Just two people holding each other in the morning light. Reminding the other that they were still here. Somehow it felt more intimate than anything they'd ever done.

"Wanna get breakfast and walk the dog before we have to go unload boxes?" She rubbed her nose against his.

Luca's lips brushed hers. "Sounds like a great plan."

* * *

"I am more than capable of lifting boxes." Therese crossed her arms and put a playful pout on her lips.

"I know, Rese." Seth gave her a wink as he and Luca started back out the door with two moving dollies.

Wren looked at the first box, labeled baby's bedroom, picked it up and passed it to Therese.

"You giving me this one because it isn't too heavy?" Therese hefted the box and started toward the bedroom as Wren grabbed another.

"No. Just grabbing the first one." It was mostly true. The box wasn't heavy, but it wasn't light, either. They set them down in what would be the nursery. "Do you want to start unpacking some things or wait until everything is up here?"

The men were bringing up the stuff, but there was no reason Wren couldn't do more than just put boxes in rooms. Assuming that was what Therese wanted.

Therese looked at the room. "It is probably a good idea to get Seth's and my room set up first. Given that this little bit won't be here for months. Still…" she looked around the room "…we aren't moving our bed over until tomorrow. Not like we're sleeping here tonight."

"So…" Wren could see the hint in Therese's gaze. She wanted to unpack the baby's room.

"The baby's stuff has been in boxes all this time." Therese looked at the corner where the crib was. "Wanna help me put it together?"

"Sure." Wren headed over to the crib box and

took a look at the side. "Says we need a screwdriver." Before the frown she saw materializing on Therese's face could form, Wren popped up. "I'll grab my toolbox. Give me just a second."

Therese clapped. "I'll get the rest of the baby's boxes ready."

Wren ran up to her place and headed back down with the whole box. Never knew what you might need in a pinch.

"Glad you have that. Ever put together a crib?" Therese had used scissors to open the box and had the pieces out on the floor.

"Nope. I'm not really maternal." Wren shrugged; kids were nice. But she'd never really gotten to be one. What did she know about raising children? Nothing.

"You don't have to want kids." Therese pulled the crib rails up. "It says we start with these."

"I didn't say I don't want them. I just…" Wren blew out a breath. "I wasn't really a kid."

"Geniuses are kids, too." Therese winked. "So you were, by definition, a child."

There was something in the way Therese emphasized the last few words. Something Wren couldn't quite place.

"Not really." Wren looked over the instructions and grabbed the pieces for the next step. "I mean, I didn't play. Or have toys or picture books. Never did the macaroni art or any art for that matter."

"Did you want to?"

"Want to what?" Wren stuck her tongue out while

she slid piece four into piece five. Sticking her tongue out wasn't strictly necessary, but it felt right.

"Play, Wren? Run your fingers through finger paint? Play make-believe or with dolls or with medical sets? You know, prep for the big role you'd take on. I played doctor, though honestly it was mostly just giving pretend shots to my parents."

That must have been nice. Wren could not even imagine asking her parents to play pretend.

"Well, I never planned to be a doctor. At least not as a little kid. So playing doctor wouldn't have really made sense." She slid the next pieces together. "I told Luca that a while ago."

"Most kids play doctor and never become one. Wait." Therese's gaze was rooted to Wren. "Never planned. What did you want to be?"

"Marine biologist was the dream. I mean as much of a dream as a sixteen-year-old college graduate can have."

"Why didn't you do that?" Therese's hand lay on top of her barely showing baby bump. The protective mother.

"My brother died. Life got unsettled after that." Wren slid another piece together. "It was easier to follow my parents' path. Took a while for me to figure out that I was not going into neuro. They were not pleased." Wren let out a laugh. That was an understatement but still the truth. "But plastics is the best medical place for me. Things change, and I am pretty good at finding the bright side." She looked up, stunned to see Therese's frown. "You okay?"

Her hand was running over her belly, her eyes wide. She nodded. "Yeah, I'm fine. Just stunned that your parents didn't let you play or even choose your own path. Did you get the boxes unloaded, Luca?"

Wren turned and beamed at Luca, who also looked like he had a frog stuck in his throat.

He shook his head. "There are few more to go. I was just checking on you two. You disappeared."

"Therese wanted help setting up the crib." Wren pointed to the partially done crib. "Once it's done, decor time? Maybe?"

"For someone who is not maternal, I appreciate your willingness to help with the nursery." Therese swallowed.

"Always happy to help." Wren grinned, not quite sure why Luca and Therese looked like she'd said something so off.

She hadn't said she loved him. Three days. Three days of perfection. Except...

Luca mentally shook himself. He needed to focus on the chart in front of him. Lena was making amazing progress. She was brighter today. Almost bubbly as she showed off her newest art to Therese.

Like Wren. Finding the bright spot.

Luca still couldn't shake the words she'd said so unconsciously to Therese. *Plastics is the best medical place.*

Not the place she was meant to be. But the best medical place.

If Ronan hadn't died. If he hadn't cosigned the loan. There was no way to know what would have been. So he had to find the bright spot. That was what Wren found. Always.

Was that why she'd let him back in after he'd been a right ass? He was grateful for the second chance, but he didn't want to be another bright spot she forced herself to find. Another path she accepted.

"Luca." Therese's voice pulled him from his unsettling woolgathering. "You have to see this painting."

Luca walked over, happy for the distraction. It was the piece Lena had shown Wren a few weeks ago. But now it was hanging in a proper gallery.

"My agent got it listed. I stole Wren's name for it. *Shadowed Storms.*" Lena looked at the image on her screen. "There have been several offers on it so far. Might even go up for auction. That'll be a first in my career."

"That is wonderful, Lena."

"A bright spot in the storm, as Wren is so fond of saying." Lena beamed. "Well, she doesn't say exactly that, but it is the general feeling."

It was. Wren pushed past the negative. Looked for the glimmer of good. But was it what she really wanted? He wasn't sure.

And worse, he wasn't sure she knew. She'd done it for so long it was simply second nature.

But that was a problem for another time. "In more wonderful news, I am not sure there is much left for you here. I think this is your last session with us."

"Yeah." Lena looked at her hand. "I figured this day was coming. Any chance you know if Dr. Freson is around? I wanted to show her the picture hanging for people to see."

She would love that. "She's in her office. I'll call to let the office assistant know you're heading that way."

"Thanks." Lena signed the final discharge papers on the tablet, then headed out.

"Wren is going to love seeing that canvas hanging." Therese ran a hand over her growing belly.

"Yeah. Do you think Wren is happy?" The question was out, and he wasn't sure what to do with it. He also didn't like the look on Therese's face or the fact that she hadn't immediately said, *Of course she's happy.*

"Why are you asking?" Therese let out a heavy breath.

"We haven't had a fight. Or rather we did, all my fault, but she said something while helping with your crib—"

"About not knowing if she could raise a child because she'd never been one?"

Luca blinked. "No. Though there is a more than enough to unpack in that statement."

"Genius sounds great, on paper." Once more Therese's hands ran along her belly. "But I think in reality…" Her words died away, and there was sadness there.

The same ache had hit his chest when he'd heard Wren's statement.

"If your child had that label, you and Seth would treat them very differently than Wren's parents treated her. I know you had a loving family, though Seth's indicated his was less than perfect. Neither Wren nor I had parents that put us first." Luca waited a second, but Therese didn't say anything else. "You didn't answer my question. Think she's happy?"

"I don't know the answer." Therese offered him a kind smile. "I like Wren. A lot. But I have never heard someone say something so tragic, so easily, then just mention that she looks on the bright side. I am not saying she is unhappy."

"Just that she doesn't know what she missed out on?" Luca knew what she'd missed. Playing mermaid at the pool. Cuddling stuffed animals. First crushes. Sleepovers.

Therese shrugged. "Yeah."

"Did you see Lena's picture?" Wren was bright as she walked into the therapy room. "I mean, wow! Should I call it a picture? Painting on canvas? I never did much art stuff."

Therese's eyes hit his.

Had she wanted to do art stuff? There were tons of places around San Diego. He could see about an outing. Would see.

"I think artwork, painting or picture work." Luca kissed her cheek. "Though I admit that I don't have a lot of experience with what Lena does."

"She is magnificent." Wren grinned. "I am tempted to go to the auction. Run the price up.

Though I would probably have to force you to come, my checkbook is not going to get me past the entrance." She held up a hand. "Only joking, of course."

It was a joke. One he easily recognized. But her dark gaze held just a hint of uncertainty. An uncertainty that he'd put there. Mentally kicking himself wouldn't do any good, but his brain was adept at self-flagellation.

"We could go." Luca shrugged. "I mean there is a place for it in the living room."

He heard Therese gasp.

"And art appreciates." It was a good investment. Wren's eyes were huge. "We can't do that."

"We could, actually." Luca raised his brows. "Easily."

She waved away the words. "I *mean,* it belongs in a museum, Luca." She looked at her watch. "I have a few minutes and was going to grab coffee. Want one?"

Luca had a few minutes, plus he wanted to run the date idea by her. "Sure."

"I really was just kidding about the painting, Luca." Wren's words struck his heart.

"I know. And I know that it's going to take time, but seriously, honey, I know you aren't thinking like that. But I still think we should bid on it because it does belong in a museum, and maybe one day it can be loaned there, but no museum is buying her work. Not yet." Though given Lena's ability, he didn't doubt that the day was coming when that happened.

"You." Wren hit his hip.

"What?"

"You should bid on it. If you want to. Not we. I wasn't kidding when I said there was no way they'd let me in." She stepped into line at the coffee shop.

He was going to find a way to make sure she understood it was *we*. From now on, for as long as she wanted, they were a pair.

"Shifting the topic, want to go on a date?"

Wren crossed her arms. "Of course, but why do I feel like this is not our standard make dinner or order it in and watch a movie? With your popcorn machine."

He put an arm around her shoulder. "You really love that machine."

She didn't even try to hide the glee in her eyes. "It is one of your best qualities." She stepped up to the counter and ordered her coffee and his and quickly paid for both.

He wanted to argue that she didn't need to do it. Didn't need to prove anything to him, but he wasn't shifting the conversation there. "So, is that a yes? A date that doesn't involve my popcorn machine?"

She giggled. "All right." Her pager went off, and she lifted her coffee. "Tonight?"

"Might take me a few days to get the idea together." He wasn't sure where the creative shops were. He'd find them, but it might take a little time.

"So, what I am hearing is tonight we *can* have popcorn."

He playfully rolled his eyes to the ceiling. "Yes, tonight we can have popcorn."

CHAPTER FIFTEEN

"NOT SURE WHERE we're going, but I love the dress code." Wren was wearing a pair of loose shorts and an old tank top. "I think this might be the most comfortable I've ever been on a date." She laughed. "I guess there isn't much to judge that on."

Luca's shoulders tensed, just a bit.

"Seriously." She leaned over the car's console and kissed his cheek. "Where are we going?"

"I told you." He took her hand, kissing her fingers. "It's a surprise."

Wren looked around. "Sometime we should do a date where you show me around the city. And we have to go to a ball game."

"That can be arranged. I haven't been to a Padres game in years. Want to sit in a box?"

Wren shook her head, uncomfortable with the ease he now discussed his ability to buy what he wanted. He said he trusted her. She wanted to believe him.

There is no reason not to.

But there was something holding her back. A hesitation. Fear that it was a trick? Her parents had tricked her brother and manipulated her, but that wasn't what was happening. Still, the shift seemed so quick.

Too quick.

She wanted him to be open, but she'd meant it when she said she didn't care about his money.

"No. I want to sit in the nosebleeds. I never got to do that with Ronan. He used to talk about sitting at the top of stadium in New York. The very last row. He claimed they were the best seats."

Luca chuckled. "I promise you they are not the best seats to see the game. But they are the best to have a good time in. We can always do both."

"True." They pulled into the parking lot for a small building that just said Pottery.

"Ta-da." Luca put the car in Park.

Wren looked at the nondescript building, then back at Luca. "Are we doing pottery?"

"Yeah. I thought it would be fun. Try something new."

Wren shrugged. "All right." She had no interest in messing with clay, but if he wanted to, then she'd happily follow along.

He opened his door, then ran around and got hers, too.

"It makes me feel fancy when you do that," she said, "though I am not dressed fancy."

"When we head to the Patron Banquet at the aquarium, you will be fancy." He kissed her cheek. "But you are always fancy to me, love."

He'd not put any pressure on her saying the words. He still told her loved her, and each time she wanted to say it back. Wanted to jump into his arms, pull him tight and whisper it in his ear.

So why don't I?

"Wait until you see the dress I got." It was a mermaid dress that hugged her in all the right places. Started off pink at the top and blended into a blue green at the bottom. She'd found it at a consignment store and nearly cried when it was her size.

"I look forward to it." He gripped her hand, and they walked into the pottery studio.

"Dr. McDonnell?" An older Black woman stepped around the corner.

"Yes, but please call me Luca. Are you Libby?"

"That is me." She held out her hand, and Luca took it quickly. Then Wren did the same. "And you must be Dr. Freson."

"Just Wren is fine."

The woman was beaming at her. Wren wasn't sure why the excitement in Libby's eyes sent a shiver down her back. They were here for Luca.

"I hear that you've never done art."

Wren looked at Luca, her heart sinking. So this was a setup. It was true, she hadn't, but she also didn't have any interest in pottery. Or painting. She was fascinated with cake decorating, her social media feed was full of it. But fascinated and wanting to replicate were two different things.

Luca's grin was so big. "She hasn't. That's why I set up this treat."

Treat.

Wren looked to Luca, then at Libby. What was happening?

Libby nodded, but there was something in her gaze as she looked at Wren.

"I'm sure this will be fun." Wren wasn't sure why Luca thought this was the perfect date idea. Had she mentioned pottery? No. She was positive that wasn't something she'd discussed.

"This way." Libby led them to the back of the studio where three wheels were set up with huge blocks of clay next them. "Take a position. Today we learn to throw a pot."

Luca sat at the wheel beside her, so pleased.

Wren grabbed her clay and did her best to follow the gentle instructions Libby gave them.

"I don't think there is any salvaging this pot." Wren scrunched her nose as her pot collapsed for at least the twentieth time. "I am an unmitigated disaster for this block of clay, Libby."

"It's fine, Wren. Pottery is a skill that takes years to truly master." Libby turned her attention to Luca. "You, however, picked this up very quickly."

Luca grinned at the pot sitting on his wheel. It was a real pot. The right size and thickness. His pot had only collapsed twice. And the happiness in his face was infectious. "This is surprisingly calming."

Wren had to hold back a gasp. That was the exact opposite of the description she'd give to this activity. Her blood pressure must have risen several points over the last two hours.

"We have classes." Libby started to reach for a flyer, but Luca held up his hand.

"With my role at the hospital, it's hard to make regular classes work."

Wren bit her tongue to keep from interrupting. Saturday classes might not always work. There were hours on the weekend, and he did some shifts on Sundays, but as a physical therapist, his hours rarely went past six. He could do this, if he wanted.

"I also offer private lessons." Libby pointed to the pot. "If you work at this, I have no doubt that you would pick it up really fast."

"I appreciate the vote of confidence but..." Luca's gaze hit Libby's. "What do I do with the pot now?"

"That is up to you. I can set it outside and let it dry, then put it in the kiln for the bisque firing. Or we can wrap it in plastic, and it will stay wet for a while so you can do more work on it."

"More work on it?" Luca looked at the pot, a gleam in his eye.

He had enjoyed this. Wren would need to reach out to Libby to find out more about private lessons. Maybe if she gifted him some lessons, he'd come back to enjoy himself.

"Sure." Libby pointed to a wall of tools that looked terrifying to Wren but must create the beautiful designs on the pieces she'd seen lining the front of Libby's studio. "You can add designs or any number of things. Or we fire this one, and then you put a glaze on it."

"Oh, like those paint-a-pottery places?" Wren

put her hand on Luca. "A friend in New York did one of those places for her bridal shower. It's fun."

Luca looked at her hand. "Do you want to glaze it?"

Taking a deep breath before she answered was the only to keep her voice level. "No. It is *your* pot. Your art."

"Sure, but we came for you."

Her gaze flicked to Libby. This was not a discussion she wanted an audience for, but here they were. "I know, but you are the one who enjoyed this activity." She squeezed his arm. "And I loved watching you enjoy it, even as I crashed my pot, over and over."

Luca looked at the busted clay on her wheel. "Well, you don't have much to work with there."

She giggled. "I do not."

He stared at his pot for a minute, then looked at Libby. "I think it's done. That sounded weird. I mean, I would know if it was done. It's a pot. It's done."

Libby waited a moment, probably trying to make sure the words he'd slipped out actually meant what he wanted them to. "You are the artist. If it feels done to you, then it is done."

Luca gave the pot one more stare. "Done."

"Perfect. I will let you know when it is ready for glazing." Libby gave Luca a bit more information, and Wren hated how he kept sending glances back at her.

It was fine that he loved this, and she'd found it frustrating as hell. She just hoped he'd realized that.

Pottery had been a huge fail. Wren had done her best, but it was clear she hadn't enjoyed it. So what was next?

"You look pensive?" Wren leaned over and kissed his cheek. A cake-decorating video was running on her phone.

"Do you want to try cake decorating?" There were classes on that. Right?

She let out a sigh and purposefully shut off her phone's screen. "That was not an answer to my question."

Luca couldn't argue that point. "You didn't enjoy pottery the other day."

A little puff of air broke through her lips.

"You don't have to lie. It was easy to see." He'd been so proud of that idea. Something fun and different. "Should we have started with painting?"

"Why are we doing art stuff? Because I liked Lena's masterpiece?" Her dark eyes were wide. Confused.

"Because you didn't get to do any of this." He let out a huff. He had all the resources he could imagine. Wren could do anything she wanted. Anything. She only had to ask.

"What?"

"You told Therese that you didn't do art or play make-believe." She'd also said that she didn't play doctor…and that it wasn't the plan. Silence hung in the air, so he pressed on, "Any interest in going back to school?" Maybe it was a weird question, but the woman loved the library. She stopped by at least once a week. If she had headphones on during a run, it was an audiobook piping through them.

Her eyes shifted, just a hair. With excitement? He thought so. All right, that made sense. She was a genius. There had to be tons of stuff she'd wanted to study that had been deemed off-limits.

Luca thought back through the books he'd seen on the floor. The fiction novels were all thrillers this week. The nonfiction books... He tried to think. What was in the stack?

She'd gone directly to the non-fiction section while he slowly roamed the stacks, trying to find anything that might call to him. He enjoyed reading, but in the week it took him to finish a book, Wren dropped through six or seven. So what was the focus this week?

Dark covers. Crowns.

"The Tudors!" He snapped his fingers.

Wren giggled. "Not sure why you're so excited about the Tudors. Suddenly have an interest in King Henry the Eighth or Elizabeth the First? Those two are the ones people are most interested in."

"Not bloody Mary?"

Wren stuck out her tongue. "I guess there is a lot of interest in her as well. Why are you asking?"

He wasn't actually interested in the Tudor Queen. "I only know her from the mirror game."

The playful look in Wren's eyes disappeared. "Mirror game?"

And the reality of why she looked confused hit his gut. "Yeah. You go into a dark bathroom with a flashlight or a candle and chant Bloody Mary." Luca put a finger on his chin. "Three times, four? I didn't play at many sleepovers, but then her ghost is supposed to come haunt you."

"Children were playing with candles in the bathroom?" The horror on her features might have been cute if it wasn't another reminder that her childhood was spent in auditoriums and classrooms, listening to lectures.

"That is what you took away from this conversation? Candles in the bathroom?"

She pulled back a little. "I mean, I never slept over. Not like the high school girls wanted the random eleven-year-old from the back of class, who always broke the curve, at their sleepover gatherings. Was it supposed to be scary? I mean, it's not like the ghost would appear."

Luca shrugged. "You so sure of that?"

"Of course."

"Come on, then." He gripped her hand, pulling her off the couch.

"Where are we going?"

"To get a candle. I have some in the closet in case of power outages." It was a silly game, but spooky stories were rites of passage.

She raised a brow. "I thought you also did this with flashlights."

"Yes." He leaned over, his lips just above hers. "But we are adults. I think we can be trusted with candles." He brushed her lips. Then pulled a candle down from the shelf, along with the matches he kept next to them.

He opened the guest bathroom door, lit the candle and handed it to her.

Wren hesitated. "I just go in and say, Bloody Mary, three or four times…" she grinned, mimicking his uncertainty "…and come back out. Really?"

"Why the hesitation?" He raised both his eyebrows. "You scared?" He made sure to keep his voice playful, far from the accusatory tones he remembered growing up.

She took the candle and looked at the door. "In the dark?"

"Yep, oh, and you put the light just below your face. If it was a flashlight, it went under your chin, but with the candle, I don't recommend it." He kissed the top of her forehead, then gestured to the bathroom. "You going?"

Wren rolled her eyes to the ceiling, then stepped into the bathroom. He closed the door and stepped back. This was ridiculous.

It took just a moment before she swung the door open, a little faster than he'd expected.

"All right. Fine. I can see why that might be scary for kids." She blew out the candle. "The face in the mirror is yours, but it's creepy. No ghost but unsettling."

"Exactly!" Luca's fingers brushed hers as he took

the candle. "But hey, now you know what a lot of American preteens did at sleepovers. We could always walk down to Seth and Therese's place and see if they want to play light as a feather, stiff as a board. Get the full experience."

"I am not even going to ask what that is." Then her lips were on his, arms wrapped around his neck. When she pulled back, there was a look in her gaze that sent a shiver down his spine.

"That was fun. Creepy but fun. However…" she tapped her temple "…steel trap here, so why were you looking so pensive?"

Luca squeezed her tightly. "I hate how much you missed." He laid a finger over her lips to stop the argument he suspected was coming. "There are adventures and activities that you should have had. So I tried the pottery, which I loved and you hated."

"I didn't hate it."

Luca raised a brow.

"I liked watching you do it, but the clay got under my nails, and it just felt icky." She looked over her shoulder at the mirror. "I have no interest in arts and crafts. I mean, I love watching cake-decorating videos but I don't want to do that. And to head off your other questions, my student loans keep the very idea of going back to school off the table."

Maybe the dream of marine biology hadn't died. Not completely at least. Wren was only twenty-six. Sure, she had med school and residency behind her, but lots of people walked away from careers for another life.

The loan was something he could take care of. Wipe it out of existence and let her chase whatever she wanted. Have the life she wanted. The life she deserved.

CHAPTER SIXTEEN

EDDIE LET OUT a wheeze as he stepped off the bottom step of the stair simulator they kept in the physio room.

"All right, let's go up again." The man was making good progress, but good progress when you'd been nearly burned to a crisp still left a lot of room between now and whatever his final new normal was.

"You suck, Doc. You know that."

"I've heard it a time or two. Now come on."

Eddie threw him a glare, then started up the steps. Glares were motivators. Luca could work with glares.

"I saw Dr. Freson today." Eddie went up another step.

"I'm sure she's happy with the progress of your burns." He'd heard from Wren that Eddie needed another surgery. Already scheduled for next week. From what she'd said, Eddie had not taken the news well.

"Sure, my skin is ready for the next round of plastic surgery to make it less hideous, maybe." Eddie reached the top step and turned to head down the stairs. "But she wasn't in my room to talk about the upcoming surgery."

Luca watched the steady but trembling steps Eddie took. *Can he go one more round on the stairs or is it time to shift to hand workouts?*

"What did you two discuss?" If Luca kept him talking, Eddie might turn around on the bottom step and head back up. Probably not. But it happened.

"Tudor England." Eddie let out a wince as he hit the bottom step. "One more, I assume?"

Luca nodded. If Eddie felt like it was possible, then it was. But he took a step closer just in case. "Why Tudor England?"

"Oh, I wrote my PhD on Mary the First and Elizabeth the First's relationship. Dr. Freson is shockingly knowledgeable on the topic."

The books on her floor this week. All Tudor dynasty books. Suddenly the image of his patient, Mrs. Demer, holding a thriller novel while waiting for her session flashed in his brain. Wren had headed straight to the librarian's desk and asked for thriller titles. He'd assumed she wanted something new. She did…because of Mrs. Demer.

A few weeks ago, the books were all art history. Which was certainly for Lena.

And her sudden interest in the Tudors… Eddie.

"Yeah, she is a font of information on many topics." Luca crossed his arms as Eddie hit the top step. But what did she like?

Did she even know?

No.

His stomach sank as the truth pushed into him. Wren spent her life making others happy. The genius people pleaser. The ray of sunshine who hid her emotions behind a brilliant smile.

"She was talking to me about the Bloody Mary mirror game." The words brought a grin to Eddie's tired features.

"I informed her of the game. Last night actually." And she hadn't mentioned this week's books were for Eddie. That she was reading to benefit her patients and other long-term residents; Mrs. Demer was here for a broken hip.

"Yeah. She told me. I guess she wasn't allowed to sleep over as a kid." Eddie hit the bottom step.

That wasn't quite the truth, but Luca wasn't going to add to anything that Wren hadn't shared.

"It was nice to have someone to talk to about it. My ex—" Eddie let out a breath. "She wasn't interested in my work. I think she thought marrying a college professor without tenure was beneath her."

Luca didn't know what to say to that.

"It's wild how easy that is to see now that we aren't engaged." Eddie looked at his scarred hand. "The red flags were there."

Luca nodded. He'd missed a lot of red flags with Madeline. Things that were very obvious once she wasn't in the picture. It lessened the hurt, though it did not remove it entirely. Only time healed that wound.

Eddie stepped to the ground and looked back at the steps. "I can't do it again, man."

Luca didn't try to hide his grin. "You did it two

times more than I wanted you to. I think that progress is fantastic."

Eddie rolled his eyes, but there was no anger in his expression. "I feel like I got had."

"Nope. You were just very involved in the discussion and working on yourself. And you stopped when your body was ready. That is exactly what you should do." The door to the room opened, and the porter and Wren walked in together.

"Looks like my ride is here." Eddie gave Wren a quick grin, then settled into the chair. "One day soon, I am going to walk next to the porter back to my room."

Wren gave Eddie one of her brilliant smiles. "One day, you are going to walk into this room from outside the hospital."

"One day." Eddie nodded, but the grin faltered just a bit.

Wren clearly clocked it. "What if I stop by before my shift ends and we talk the odds of Elizabeth's involvement in Wyatt's Rebellion?"

"Oh, that discussion will take at least half an hour. And that is just for the overview." The historian's face was brighter than Luca had seen it in the weeks he'd known him.

"I will make the time." Wren gave a quick goodbye, then turned her attention to Luca. "I got you a coffee." She passed him the cup. "Decaf since it's already past three."

"Decaf?" He looked at the cup in horror.

She giggled. "Of course not."

Luca let out a playful sigh as he brought the lid to his lips. "Thank you. And was Elizabeth involved in the rebellion?" He didn't really care, but he was curious what her response might be.

"No one knows for sure. She was found innocent but…" Wren shrugged "…who knows? The books I read on the subject were rather dry."

There it was. The admission and his entry point. "So why read them?"

The pure shock on her face was enough for him to register that she truly didn't understand the reason for the question. "Eddie is a Tudor historian. I mentioned that last night. Oh, actually, I think you started ghost talk, and that distracted me."

"And the thrillers?"

"Mrs. Demer reads two to three a day. Claims that there is only so much television one can watch, and she refuses to keep it on all the time. I wish I had more patients that felt that way. The faster they're up and moving, the faster they can leave." She sipped her drink. "Why are you asking about Mrs. Demer's reading habits?"

Did she really not understand what she was doing? Was it so ingrained in her to follow through with what made others happy that she didn't recognize what her decisions meant?

"I am not questioning Mrs. Demer's reading choices. I am questioning yours."

"Mine."

"Yours." Luca lifted the coffee to his lips. "What does my love enjoy reading?"

"Are you looking for a book to get me?" She tapped his shoulders, but there was color rising in her cheeks. This struck an uncomfortable nerve.

Which meant he was on the right path.

"Come on, Wren, you've spent more time in libraries than anyone I know. What section is your favorite? What is your favorite genre? What authors do you have to read the second their books are released?"

"I don't know." The words slipped from her perfect lips, and her eyes widened. "I mean, of course I know. I love books."

He didn't doubt that. Luca also knew she looked for ways to please others. She'd claimed she'd chosen San Diego. But also mentioned that Dr. Link's family was fully settled in New York. Wren would never have made the choice to make her colleague leave the city. So she was here. And he was grateful for it.

But it wasn't a true choice.

She took a deep breath. "I don't know what my favorite is. What I know is that I love books, and I love you."

Words he'd ached to hear drop from her tongue. Words his heart broke to hear right now. But it felt like she was shifting the subject. And giving another person what they wanted instead of answering what she needed.

"Wren."

Therese walked in, a patient walking with a cane beside her. A very proud patient.

Wren looked at Luca, but all his words were stuck. Why had she said it? Did she really mean it?

"Enjoy the coffee." Wren held hers up and waved at Therese as she headed out.

Luca gave a thumbs-up to the patient, but his eyes darted back to the door. He'd missed so many red flags with Madeline. What if he was overlooking a few now?

No. That couldn't be true.

So why couldn't he stop the panic settling in his stomach? Why was it so hard for her to identify what she liked for herself?

And is she saying I love you because it's what I want to hear?

There was no way to ignore the somersaults Wren's stomach kept doing as she stood in her apartment. The executive freeze was dropping—again. She was mentally pushing it back, but it was going to fail.

It always failed.

She'd told Luca she loved him. It was true. She did. But the declaration seemed so anticlimactic. No grand gesture. No giant meaning. In the moment, her brain and heart just had to have it in the world. The conversation on books was ridiculous. And sweet. And so Luca, trying to guide her to an answer about herself.

The words she'd feared releasing flowed so seamlessly into the conversation.

And he didn't look thrilled.

Nope. He'd had the same look on his face that

he'd had at Therese and Seth's apartment. The same look when pottery hadn't held any appeal for her. Disappointment.

She'd seen it in so many faces over the course of her life. The teens mad that the kid who belonged in elementary school was killing the curve in honors high school classes. The overachievers in college frustrated that she was stealing the attention because of her genius. The med school colleagues that didn't know what to do with her.

And her parents when she refused to do what they wanted and go into neurology, even after she'd done everything else asked of her. Followed their path so closely. It wasn't like she'd dropped out of med school.

She smiled and went along with what people wanted. And it was never enough. Never.

Now it was Luca. Looking at her, his jeweled gaze filled with disappointment.

He's trying to fix me.

He hasn't said that.

Does he need to?

Wren!

The mental screams seemed to echo through the apartment as she wrapped her arms around herself. He knew she didn't care about his money. It seemed to free him, which was good. But...

Now he's using it to give me experiences I missed. Poor little genius!

Her brain hammered away, chipping at her heart.

A knock at the door. Luca.

She swallowed and turned. He'd come in. He had a key. She wanted him here.

And I want him gone.

Why would her brain not shut the hell up?

"Hey. I've got news." Luca held up a bottle of wine. The same bottle she'd opened the night they had their fight.

Why was it the same bottle?

He walked over, kissed her cheek. No words of love. No discussion of the announcement she'd made this afternoon. Was that a good thing?

No.

But he has wine.

Luca grabbed two wineglasses and got the bottle opener from her top drawer.

"Why do you have the wine I had in my refrigerator?" It was a coincidence. It was. Please.

Luca grinned as he poured two glasses and passed her one. The wine was chilled. So whatever this was, was planned. "I know you followed your parents' ideas. Med school instead of marine biology."

This again? She liked sea horses. Enjoyed reading about the ocean. The depths of it were still fully unexplored. "I was sixteen, Luca. Yes, marine biology was interesting, but I followed my own path. I have the student loans to prove it."

Would she have ended up a marine biologist if Ronan hadn't passed? Maybe. But it was just as likely that she'd have found her way to plastics. He'd pushed back on her parents, but it hardly ever worked. She wasn't sure she'd have had the strength to walk away completely.

"Sixteen." Luca chuckled. "At sixteen I was learning to drive and spending as much time away from home as possible. I was sneaking into movies with friends and going to school dances, and you were in med school."

She shrugged and looked at the wineglass. "Life of a genius."

"That is the first time I've heard you call yourself that." Luca took a step toward her.

The tag defined her. She didn't want it, but that didn't mean it wasn't true.

"Why the wine?" She took a deep breath. "Did a patient graduate physical therapy that I am not tracking?"

"The wine is for you."

She raised a brow as her stomach dived. She hadn't accomplished anything. Not recently at least. "For me?" What on earth did that mean?

"You are wrong." Luca raised his glass. "You don't have the student loans to show for med school. You are free. And I found the right bottle to celebrate. This is the one, right?"

"You paid off my student loans?" The words were barely a whisper.

"I did." He was so happy.

And she couldn't match the energy. Not yet. "Why?"

Everything hung on this answer. The world

stopped as she looked from his raised glass to the subtle frown settling into his features.

"Why?" Luca shook his head. "What do you mean why?"

"I mean why did you pay them off?" *Because you love me. Say because you love me. Let that be the reason. Not because of how I was raised or what I missed or didn't get.*

Because I love you.

She tried to will those words to come from his lips. Just those words.

"You didn't get to decide what to do. You followed your parents' outlined path." Luca set his glass down.

She hadn't, though. Not completely. Why couldn't he see that?

"Wren, you're free to do—"

She held up her hand. "No. No. No." She set her glass next to his. "No."

An uncomfortable laugh erupted from her throat. This was not happening. She'd told him she loved him this afternoon. Unceremoniously but still. That should be what they were talking about. Instead, he was wiping away hundreds of thousands of dollars of medical school debt without even talking to her.

"How did you even get the information?"

His cheeks colored. "Made a few calls. That isn't what's important right now."

"I disagree."

Luca took a step toward her, "Wren, that debt is keeping you from going back to school."

Back to school? She blinked as the words she'd planned to say evaporated from her mind. "Luca."

"It is not off the table now. It is squarely on the table." He lifted his glass. "To new beginnings."

"I told you, I don't need protecting. I don't need to be fixed. I didn't ask you to pay off my student loans."

He'd lost his mind just two weeks ago about money and people demanding it from him. Now—without asking her—he'd wiped away over two hundred thousand dollars' worth of debt.

"I am not protecting you. I am not fixing things. I mean, I am, but damn it, Wren, you've earned it."

"Why?" It felt like that word was constantly on her lips right now. "Because the poor little genius didn't get the perfect childhood? Please. You didn't get it, either. Far too many kids don't get it."

"You didn't get to find yourself." The words were out, and he snapped his lips together.

"You think I don't know myself." Wren wrapped her arms around herself. "I love you, Luca."

"Are you sure? Or are you just trying to make me happy?" He set the wineglass down. No toasts were happening tonight. "Because you are so sunny, so bright, but how much of it is what you want and how much is you pleasing everyone around you without asking for what you need? You aren't a ray of sunshine. You're a woman who marches past her pain to help others. Which is fine—if you acknowledge it. But you are burying it."

That arrow landed a direct hit.

"You used your money to push people away. And now you're using it to try to make me happy. What makes you happy, Luca? What brings joy to your life? Because you are hiding behind the wealth someone left you. Using it as an excuse to avoid people."

He flinched as her words found their mark.

"And you are hiding behind the title genius." Another direct shot. "You expect everyone to look at you that way, and you hold yourself apart."

Their last fight was loud. The people across her hall had checked on her after. This one was nearly silent. Two adults pointing out the pain they'd seen in the other but not reaching for them.

"I don't need to be fixed. And I will pay you back the loan." She hadn't wanted his money. She'd made that clear. If only he'd paid it off just because he loved her.

"Wren."

"Goodbye, Luca."

He didn't argue. Didn't hesitate to walk around her. Didn't say anything else on his march out the door.

When it was closed, she let the first tear fall.

CHAPTER SEVENTEEN

"You scowl any deeper, and even the patients won't be able to pretend to ignore it, McSteamy." Therese didn't laugh as she said the words. Some of the first she'd said to him all day.

Luca shrugged and walked over to the computer to look at the notes for his next patient.

"So we are back to the no-word responses. Wow." Therese crossed her arms.

Luca pulled up the chart but didn't feel like engaging with any of this. Not today. Three days since he'd walked out of Wren's apartment. Two days since he'd found a box of his clothes by his door. He hadn't packed her stuff yet.

And she hasn't asked. He swallowed the lump in his throat.

"She get tired of you playing master of ceremony for her life?"

"Excuse me." Luca looked at her. "What the hell is that supposed to mean?"

Therese raised her chin as she met his gaze. "You asked if she was happy."

"And you told me that you didn't know." Luca's voice was too loud. He took a deep breath. "Sorry." He turned back to the computer.

"It is not my job to know." Therese took another step toward him. "But it is yours."

"Was." Luca keyed in a few notes and pulled up Eddie's chart. The man had therapy in an hour. There were notes from Wren. Short. To the point.

The kind of notes doctors routinely left. But not Wren. She'd always expanded. Given hints on the patients' day. Any knowledge she'd learned that might help motivate them for physical therapy.

"Luca, I am not going to push this, but..." Therese ran her hand over the ever-growing baby bump. "But when we found out that Seth was the baby's father..." she let out a deep breath "...I expected a reaction from him. I didn't give him time to accept the giant life change. I put my expectations on him. It wasn't fair." She waited for a moment, but what was he to say to that? "It nearly cost us everything." Therese stood there for a second, then turned and walked away.

Luca stared at Eddie's notes for another moment. So short. No extras. Nothing that had come to define Wren.

I wasn't playing master of ceremony.

Except he had.

He bit the inside of his cheek. Therese was right. He'd seen a lack, and rather than have a discussion about it, talk with Wren about her wants, he'd just started planning.

Because she didn't tell me what she wanted.

Why would she?

That truth hit him squarely in the chest. He'd

made a huge show of not telling anyone about his money. Then flipped the switch when she didn't care about it. Trying desperately to earn what he feared wasn't freely given.

Hell, he'd planned to step away as soon as she decided she was done. Planned to be an adventure she enjoyed and then step back so she could do whatever she wanted. She'd said goodbye, and he'd followed the plan to a T.

Luca pulled at the back of his neck.

"Hey, doc." Eddie's voice hit his back. "I am not really in the mood for stairs today. In a funk."

Funks happened. And since Luca was in the deep depths of one, he could hardly fault Eddie for this one.

Pushing his own emotions away, Luca offered what he hoped was a convincing smile. "Why are you in a funk?" He waved to the porter as Eddie stood and moved to the sitting bicycle that Luca pointed to.

"Beth stopped by." Eddie sat down. "Said she was sorry."

Luca crossed his arms as he gestured for Eddie to start the bike. Madeline had never apologized. It probably never crossed her mind. He wasn't sure what he would have done had his ex-fiancée tried to walk back into his life.

"I think she expected me to be happy she came back." Eddie shifted on the seat and started pedaling. "If you and Dr. Freson hadn't talked with me over the last month, I might have been. But…"

Luca didn't interrupt. He'd heard a lot in this room. People told physical therapists all sorts of things. Some because they wanted to pass the time, some because it took their mind off the hard work, and some because they were talking to a person they knew wouldn't tell anyone.

It took a moment, but Eddie continued, "But I realize I spent all of our relationship trying to make myself worthy of her." Eddie laughed, no happiness behind it. "Which might be fine, if she didn't expect it?"

"What do you mean?" The question slipped out.

"She expected it. I wasn't good enough for her, I never would have been. But if she didn't expect it, if I was pushing myself to be worthy of her because I was worried that I wasn't good enough, it might have been all right. I think."

"No." Luca pushed the word out. "No. That wouldn't work, either. You have to know you're good enough on your own." The words were for Eddie but mostly for himself.

He'd spent his childhood trying to be enough for his parents. Only when Maude's inheritance come through had they wanted him. Then he'd used the inheritance as an excuse to hide away after Madeline's betrayal. If he didn't give anyone a chance, they'd never realize he wasn't worth it.

Wren loved him. And rather than accept the words, he'd wondered if she was saying them to make him happy.

If she'd planned to do that, she'd have said it the

moment he said it to her. Instead, she'd offered the words in a moment when she felt them.

He'd paid off her loans, granting her a freedom she'd never asked for. His soul clenched. He'd stopped by with wine. With an expectation that she'd be happy—and that he'd been worthy of her in that moment.

No one ever saw him for himself...because he didn't give them the option to.

He looked at the clock. Six hours left on this shift. Six hours until he could find her. Apologize, tell her he loved her and ask to walk beside her. Not as a master of ceremony giving her whatever he felt she missed out on. But as a partner who loved the other.

Six hours.

A lifetime away.

Wren stared at the dress in the closet. The mermaid gown she'd planned to wear to the ball. The ball taking place tomorrow night. She should be planning her hair and makeup for the evening she'd looked forward to for months.

Instead she was fingering the delicate beading. She loved the dress. Not because it was aquarium themed, though that was a nice touch. She felt perfect in it. And the second it was on, all she could think was about how Luca would love it.

And she wasn't going to get to wear it because she got mad her insanely wealthy boyfriend paid off her student loans.

Wren turned away from the dress. Maybe she

should see if the consignment shop would take it back. Surely it would sell again. But she didn't want to give it up.

She looked at the stack of books on her nightstand. Three thrillers she'd promised to talk to Mrs. Demer about and another book on the Tudor dynasty. None of which held any interest for her.

Wren crossed her arms as she looked at the books. The titles screaming at her.

Who was her favorite author?

Her favorite genre?

She pulled up the app she used to track the books she read, even though Wren knew what she was going to find. A list of books she'd read to talk to others about. Even the digital shelves she'd created were named after patients or colleagues. It was like she'd gotten out of school and continued studying. Except instead of coursework, it was books to please her patients.

"What do I like?"

This was not a hard question. Wren put her phone in her pocket and bit her lip. Luca was right. She hated the title genius. Never used it, but it was her identity. The thing that kept her separate.

Because she let it.

Luca should have talked to her. But he was right, she put others first—always. Even in her reading preferences.

She knew what she wanted. Who she wanted.

She needed to make a quick stop, then she needed to see Luca.

* * *

Wren held the books to her chest. Once she'd walked in the stacks for herself, the answer had become so obvious. She had six in her arms right now.

Stepping out of the elevator, she took a deep breath as she turned to look at his door at the end of the hall.

Take the first step, Wren.

She was meant to be in San Diego. Meant to be a plastic surgeon. Meant to help people. But there were things she'd missed. Experiences she wanted.

And she wanted them with Luca. She just had to hope he still wanted them with her. She started toward his place—only one way to find out.

The door to his apartment opened as she was halfway there, and Luca stepped out.

"Are you going someplace?" She had a plan. Sort of.

"No." Luca put his hands in his pockets and nodded toward the door. "Hippo started his tippy-tap dance. He only does that when you're on the floor."

Now or never.

"Fantasy." She stated the genre as she stepped up to him.

"What?"

"Fantasy. Epic fantasy. High fantasy. Urban fantasy. Romantasy. Low fantasy."

"What is low fantasy?"

"A story that takes place in the normal world with a few fantasy elements." She grinned and pulled a book from the bottom of her stack. "Like this one."

Luca smiled. "And the reason you have five fantasy books in your arms right now?"

"Six. I have six fantasy books in my arms right now." She pursed her lips. The conversation had already gone off the path she'd meant for it.

"Sorry, six."

"Not important. You were right, I put others first to a fault. And I did miss out on things. A lot of things. But I know myself. I am Dr. Wren Freson. A plastic surgeon who cocreated a radical new procedure that changed the treatment for burn patients. I love animated movies and fantasy novels. And I love you." There were tears coating her eyes.

"Wren."

Why had she thought it was a good idea to bring so many books? She could have made the point with one or two and easily thrown her arms around him. Instead, the stack was clumsily in her hands right now.

"I should have talked to you about what you wanted," he began. "You were right, not that I was trying to fix you, but that I hide behind my wealth. First using it to keep people away and then trying to use it to make all your dreams come true, so I was worthy of you."

"Worthy?"

Luca held up a hand. "I spent my childhood, like you, trying to prove myself. I tried everything to earn my parents' love. Madeline's. I never felt good enough. Then I fell in love with you. You are kind, intelligent, quick-witted and able to eat way more popcorn than anyone I know."

"Hey!" She sniffed as a happy tear slipped down her cheek.

"All true." He closed the small distance between them, taking the books out her hands. "I want to give you everything, Wren. Not because you missed out, though I will never forgive your parents for that, but because I love you."

"I love you, too."

EPILOGUE

"I LIKE THAT DRESS, Dr. Freson-McDonnell." Luca ran his hand over her back, kissing the top of her exposed shoulder.

Wren brushed her lips against his. She'd never get tired of hearing him call her Dr. Freson-McDonnell. "It's the same dress I wore last year." The mermaid dress was quite the statement piece.

"I know." Luca's hand traced her bare back. "I remember what happened after this event last year. I am still as excited by it as I was then. If I recall, we left the Aquarium Patron Banquet early last time."

Wren leaned her head against his shoulder. "This time we can't. We have to wait until Lena's masterpiece is revealed."

Luca shook his head. "I still think that piece looks best in our living room."

Wren hit her hip against his. "It is only on loan here for a year."

"This is so exciting." Therese walked up, Seth right behind her, head bent over his phone.

"It is." Wren looked at Seth. "He all right?"

"It's our first date night away from the baby. The sitters—"

"Are not answering their texts." Seth let out a tiny huff.

Therese playfully rolled her eyes. "I was going to say the sitters are probably enjoying playing grandma and grandpa."

Luca pressed his lips to the top of Wren's head, but she could feel the laughter he was trying very hard to hide.

"Seth is a wonderful dad." Wren didn't hold in her giggle as she watched Seth send another text to his in-laws.

Therese's gaze shifted as she starred at her husband. "Yes. He is."

"Oh!" Luca pointed to the stage. "I think it's showtime."

Lena's gaze was searching the crowd, and when it settled on them, she seemed to let out a sigh.

What a difference a year made.

Wren looked at her husband, then at Seth and Therese. From all alone, to a family of her own creating. She couldn't imagine finding a better life path.

* * * * *

Get up to 4 Free Books!

We'll send you 2 free books from each series you try PLUS a free Mystery Gift.

FREE Value Over **$25**

Both the **Harlequin Presents** and **Harlequin Medical Romance** series feature exciting stories of passion and drama.

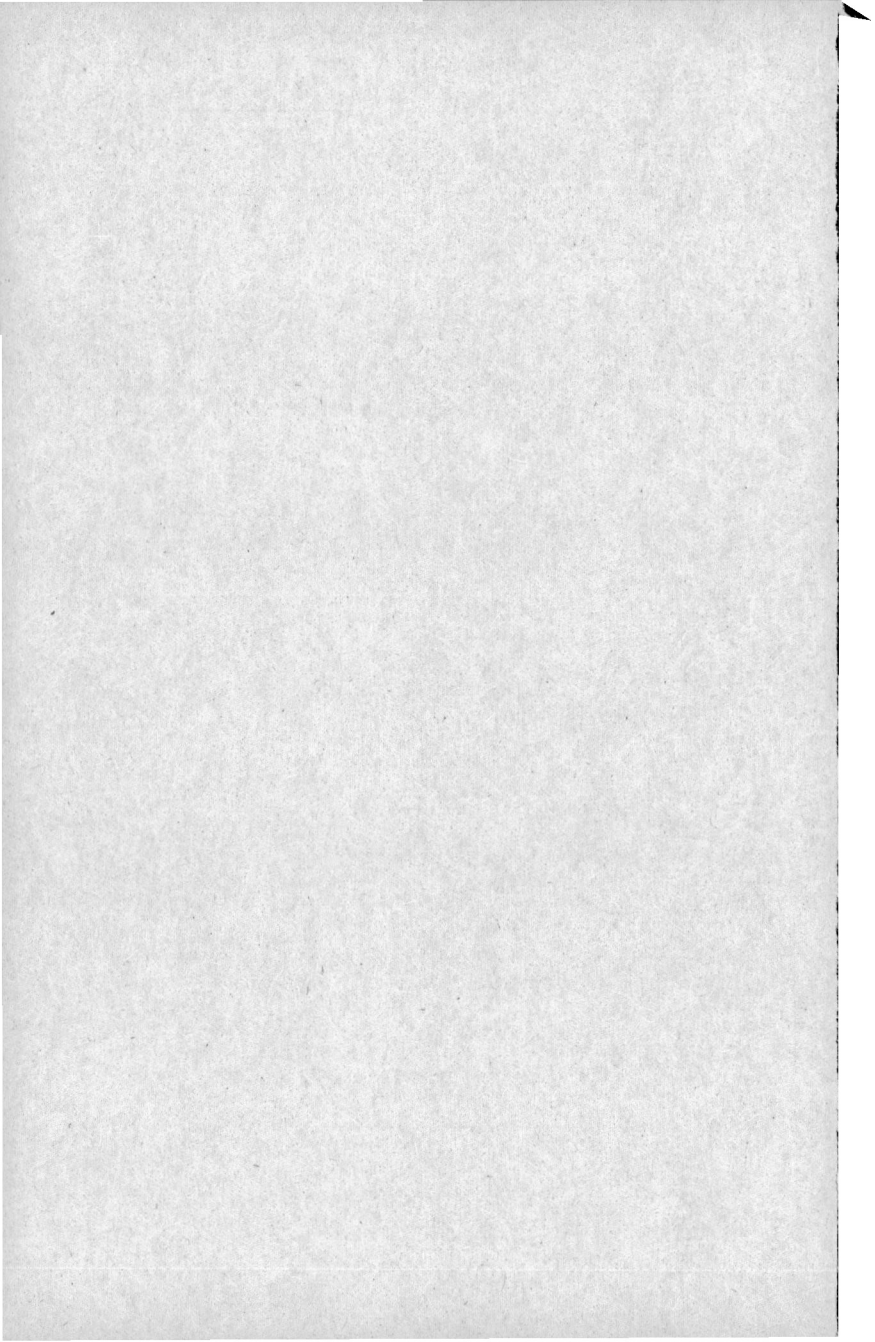